"We need to talk."

Brewer could finally catch his breath. Think about his next step. "Okay."

She walked into the kitchen, where a handyman had just arrived to fix the back door.

"I understand if you don't trust my ability to keep you safe, but—"

"Whoa," Brewer said, interrupting her. "What gives you that impression?"

She studied him as she folded her arms across her chest. "The safe house was compromised minutes after we arrived." She shrugged. "I figured after almost getting ditched back at the diner that you'd definitely want to be rid of me now."

"I'm alive because of your quick thinking," he corrected. He knew a good teammate when he encountered one. "If you hadn't jumped me, I would likely be dead right now. If anything, this has shown me that I do need someone else to have my back."

BOUNTY
HUNTED

USA TODAY BESTSELLING AUTHOR
BARB HAN

All my love to Brandon, Jacob and Tori, my three greatest loves. How did I get so lucky?

To Babe, my hero, for being my best friend, greatest love and my place to call home. I love you with everything that I am.

Harlequin®
INTRIGUE™

ISBN-13: 978-1-335-45686-1

Bounty Hunted

Copyright © 2024 by Barb Han

Harlequin Enterprises ULC
22 Adelaide St. West, 41st Floor
Toronto, Ontario M5H 4E3, Canada
www.Harlequin.com

Printed in U.S.A.

USA TODAY bestselling author **Barb Han** lives in north Texas with her very own hero-worthy husband, three beautiful children, a spunky golden retriever/standard poodle mix and too many books in her to-read pile. In her downtime, she plays video games and spends much of her time on or around a basketball court. She loves interacting with readers and is grateful for their support. You can reach her at barbhan.com.

Books by Barb Han

Harlequin Intrigue

Marshals of Mesa Point

Ranch Ambush
Bounty Hunted

The Cowboys of Cider Creek

Rescued by the Rancher
Riding Shotgun
Trapped in Texas
Texas Scandal
Trouble in Texas
Murder in Texas

A Ree and Quint Novel

Undercover Couple
Newlywed Assignment
Eyewitness Man and Wife
Mission Honeymoon

Visit the Author Profile page at Harlequin.com.

CAST OF CHARACTERS

Crystal Remington—Can this US marshal keep her witness in the program, or will he ditch her and try to do everything on his own?

Wade Brewer—Can this wounded veteran stay alive long enough to testify?

Trent Thomas—This buddy is a lifesaver, but can he be counted on?

Victor Crane—This head of a criminal organization will stop at nothing to keep Wade from testifying.

Damon O'Meara (aka Damon the Devil)—Who is he and, better yet, who does he work for?

Chapter One

Crystal Remington repositioned her black Stetson, lowering the rim, after she opened the door of the Dime a Dozen Café off I-45. She scanned the small restaurant for Wade Brewer. At six feet, four inches of solid muscle, the thirty-three-year-old former Army sergeant shouldn't be too difficult to locate against the backdrop of truckers and road-tripping families.

In the back left corner, Mr. Brewer sat with his back against the wall. His position gave him an open view of the room. As a US marshal and someone who was used to memorizing exits, Crystal appreciated the move. At his vantage point, no one would have an opportunity to sneak up on him from the side or behind.

He glanced up and then locked onto her, not bothering to motion for her to come sit down. In fact, he looked downright put out by her presence. What the hell?

Tight chestnut-brown-colored hair clipped close to a near-perfect head and a serious face with hard angles and planes, she didn't need to look at a picture to verify her witness's identity. This was the man she was scheduled to meet. After deciding she wasn't a threat, he leaned forward over the table and nursed a cup of coffee as she walked over to join him.

He picked up a sugar packet and twisted it around his

fingers. "Marshal Remington, I'm guessing." Most would consider him physically intimidating, but she'd grown up around a brother and a pair of cousins similar in size, so it didn't faze her.

"That would make you Wade Brewer." Crystal sat down, then signaled for the waitress before refocusing on Brewer. Even with facial scars from an explosion during his time in the service, the man was still beautiful. "Ready for the check so we can get out of this fishbowl and I can get you to a safe place?"

"Do I look like I need your help?" he shot back with daggers coming from his eyes. She wasn't touching that question. "Remind me why I agreed to this when I'm fully capable of taking care of myself?"

Crystal waved off the smiling waitress who was unaware of the tension at the table. And then she turned all her attention to her witness. "First of all, two of the people I love most in this world are lying in hospital beds fighting for their lives while I'm sitting here with you, so have a little respect."

Brewer didn't flinch. Instead, the most intense pair of steel-gray eyes studied her. The unexplained fear that he might pull something like this had been eating at her since she'd learned about his background. Tough guys like him generally didn't go around asking others for help. They handled life on their own terms and, generally speaking, did a bang-up job of it. She'd dismissed her worry as paranoia. Then there was the fact of her grandparents' serious car accident that had been weighing heavily on her mind. Didn't bad events usually occur in threes? If that was the case and her witness decided to bolt, she had one more to go. Lucky her. "Now that we have that fact out of the way, you are the key to locking away a major criminal who—"

"Is currently in jail," he interrupted without looking away from the rim of his cup.

From here on out, Wade was Brewer to Crystal just like everyone else she referred to. Using last names was a way to keep a distance from people. First names were too personal.

"And has a very long reach on the outside with two lieutenants and more foot soldiers ready to kill on command than you can count on both hands." She needed to get him out of this café and on the road to Dallas if they were going to get there in time to pick up the key to the town house tonight. "Why are we talking about this? I thought this issue had already been decided. It was my understanding that you agreed to enter into my protective custody. Has something changed that I haven't been informed of since six a.m.?"

"I've had time to sit here and think." Brewer took a sip of black coffee, unfazed by the emotions building inside her and emanating from her in palpable waves. "Maybe it's time to change my mind."

"Why is that, Mr. Brewer? What possible thought could you have had that would cause you to do an about-face right now?" If he said the reason had to do with her being a woman, she might scream. She'd come across perps who'd believed they could outrun or outshoot her due to her having two X chromosomes. They'd been wrong. If that was the case with Brewer, she could assure him that she was just as capable as any man to do the job or she wouldn't be here in the first place. Brewer didn't give her an indication this was the issue, but she'd come up against this particular prejudice a few too many times in the past and it always set her off.

To his credit, Brewer didn't look her up and down. Instead, he stared into his cup. "It's simple. I'll be able to stay on the move a lot easier if I'm alone. Being on the move doesn't make me a sitting duck."

"I can offer a stable safe house, Mr. Brewer."

The look he gave said he wasn't buying it. "You have no guarantees." Didn't he really mean to say she wasn't strong enough to cover him if push came to shove?

"Not one witness to date has died while following the guidelines under the protection of a US marshal," she pointed out. "I can't say the same for folks who decided they could do it themselves." She folded her arms across her chest and sat back in her chair. "Our track record speaks for itself."

Brewer didn't seem one bit impressed. The terms *dark* and *brooding* came to mind when describing him.

She needed to take another tack, offer a softer approach. "First of all, I want to thank you for your service to this country." She meant every word. "And I realize your training provides a unique skill set that most who come under my protection don't possess." Pausing for effect would give him a few seconds to process the compliment and, maybe, soften him up a little. "I have no doubt you were very good at your job, Sergeant. But make no mistake about it—my training is suited to this task. And I'm damn good at my job. If you have any doubts, feel free to contact my supervisor or any of the other marshals I've worked with over the years. This isn't my first rodeo."

He dismissed her with a wave of his hand, which infuriated her.

Taking a calming breath, she started again. "If the fact

I'm a woman bothers you, say so upfront and let's get it out of the way."

His face twisted in disgust. "I've served alongside a few of the most talented soldiers in the Army, who happened to wear bras. The fact you do has no bearing on my decision whether or not to strike out on my own."

Embarrassed, heat crawled up her neck, pooling at her cheeks. She cleared her throat, determined not to let this assignment go south. "You have no reason to trust me other than the badge I wear. You don't know me from Adam. I get that. Not to mention your military record is impeccable. If we were at war, you'd be the first person I turned to. This situation is stateside, and you have no authority here."

"I have a right to defend myself," he countered.

"Same as every citizen," she pointed out. No doubt he packed his own weapons, not that he needed a license to carry any longer. Scooting her chair closer to the table, she leaned in and lowered her voice. "Did you take care of your aunt?"

"Yes, ma'am. She has been relocated to a secure location," he said. Taking care of his elderly aunt had been his first priority after Victor Crane had been taken into custody and was the reason they were meeting north of Houston, his home city. "Without your help, by the way."

"Fair enough." Crystal could see she was losing him. Was it time to cut bait? Leave him on his own? The way she saw it, there wasn't much choice. His mind seemed made up. Then again, there was no harm in trying. She'd throw out a Hail Mary anyway and see if it worked. "At least make the drive to Dallas with me. Consider changing your mind about protective custody. What's the worst that can happen?"

He flashed eyes at her.

She put a hand up to stop him from commenting. "How about we get inside my vehicle and you can consider your options on the highway heading north?" she said. "You change your mind, I'll personally drop you off anywhere you request. No questions asked."

Brewer gave her a dressing down with his steel gaze. If he was testing her, she had no intention of backing down.

With the casual effort of a Sunday-morning stroll, he shifted gears, picked up his mug and drained the contents. After reaching into his front pocket and peeling off a twenty, he slapped it onto the table, shouldered his military-issue backpack, then stood. "Let's go."

A celebration was premature. Crystal stood up, turned around, and walked out of the diner, keeping an eye out to make sure no one seemed interested in what they were doing. She didn't like meeting this close to Galveston, Brewer's childhood home, or Houston, where he currently resided. Victor Crane would no doubt have someone on his or her way down to make certain Brewer couldn't testify. With a pair of loyal lieutenants, Crane wouldn't even have to make the call himself if Brewer's name got out as a witness. He'd been Crane's driver, so the odds of that happening were high now that Brewer had disappeared.

He followed her to her government-issue white sedan parked closest to the door without taking up an accessible parking spot. She half expected him to keep walking right on past and was pleasantly surprised when he stopped at the passenger door.

It was too early to be excited. She'd given him the out to change his mind anytime during the ride to Dallas in order to convince him to get into the car.

"I should probably hit the men's room before we continue north," he said, breaking into her small moment of victory like rain on parade day.

"All right." On a sharp sigh, Crystal took the driver's seat, figuring it was a toss-up at this point as to whether or not he would return. She tapped her thumb on the steering wheel after turning on the engine as Brewer headed inside the restaurant. What was he going to do? Sneak out the bathroom window to throw her off the trail for a few minutes? Were negotiations over? His mind made up?

She'd give him five minutes before she gave up and called it in.

BREWER CONTEMPLATED DITCHING the marshal for two seconds in the bathroom. Getting far away from Galveston and Houston was a good idea. Dallas? Was it his best move? He'd only been out of the military for six months now and hadn't come home to a warm welcome in his former hometown other than his aunt despite his service to his country.

In all honesty, he'd brought the town's reaction on himself. He'd barely graduated high school due to the number of fistfights he'd been in. He'd worked two jobs to help provide for his elderly aunt, who was technically his great-aunt, which had tanked his grades. He could have been more focused in school, except that he'd hated every minute of sitting in class. Before he'd shot up in height, he'd been bullied. And then, he'd gotten angry. The football coach, in an attempt to court him, had given Brewer permission to use the weight room before school, which he'd done religiously to bulk up and then use his newfound muscles to punish. By junior year, he'd taken issue with anyone who'd looked sideways at him and had the power to back it up.

And he'd done just that a few too many times for the principal's liking and pretty much everyone else in town whose kid he'd beaten up.

The military had given him a purpose and an outlet for all his anger, not to mention a target to focus on. He'd gone from hating the world and blaming everyone for his hard-luck upbringing to being able to set it all aside and compartmentalize his emotions. His childhood had had all the usual trappings that came with a drunk for a father who apparently couldn't stand the sight of his own child. As for his mother, she'd been a saint to him until she'd up and disappeared. The Houdini act had made Daniel Brewer hate his son even more. The man could rot in hell for all Brewer cared after what he'd ultimately done. As far as his mother went…what kind of person left a five-year-old behind to live with a drunk? Her sainthood had been short-lived as far as he was concerned. It had died along with all his love for her.

Brewer fished his burner cell out of his pocket. He fired off a text to his buddy to say this was him on a new number and to pick up. Then, Brewer put the phone to his left ear and made a call. The burner phone was new since he'd turned his old one over to the US Marshals Service for safekeeping. It was too late to regret the move now.

His buddy picked up on the second ring. "Trent, hey, it's me."

"Dude, I tried to call you." Trent Thomas breathed heavy like he was in the middle of a run. "What happened to your phone?"

"I borrowed this one." He hoped Trent wouldn't ask any more questions. They'd been military buddies early on in Brewer's career, Trent having been the closest thing to a friend in basic training when they'd both had their backsides handed to them.

A disgruntled grunt came through the line. "I had no idea what that bastard was really up to, Brew."

"Figured you didn't," Brewer reassured his buddy. The two had gone to the same middle school, high school, and boot camp. They hadn't really gotten to know each other until the latter. They forked in different directions after basic.

Then Trent had been a godsend when Brewer had medically boarded out of the Army. He'd been the first to make calls to find work for Brewer, work that had given him a reason to keep going after his life-changing injury. And now the job put his life in jeopardy. There was no way Trent could have known Crane wasn't the head of a legitimate company as they'd been told. Brewer's buddy would never do that to him.

"I feel like a real jerk for putting you in that position, dude. Especially after what you've been through and all."

"Don't sweat it," Brewer reassured. "Besides, this'll all be over in two shakes, and I'll be on the hunt for a new job."

"What can I do to help?"

He knew Trent would come through. "I need a place to hide out for a few days until I can figure out my next move. Somewhere off the grid, if you know what I mean."

The line went quiet for a few seconds that felt like minutes as Brewer turned on the spigot to wash his hands.

"I can help with that, Brew. No problem." He rattled off coordinates that Brewer entered into his cell after telling his friend to hold so he could dry his hands.

"I'll owe you big-time for this, Trent."

"Consider it payback for the position I put you in," Trent

said with a voice heavy with remorse. He wasn't normally an emotional guy, so the intensity registered as odd.

After what he'd been through in the past twenty-four hours that had led him to standing in front of a bathroom mirror in a roadside café made him more than ready to get off the grid, where he could catch his meals and cook his own food. Civilization wasn't as civilized as he'd wanted it to be.

"I'll be in touch when I can." He ended the call on the off chance someone was listening. Freedom was near. All he had to do was ditch the marshal sitting in the parking lot and get on the road.

After entering the coordinates into his map feature, he smiled. This place was so remote, all that showed on the screen was a patch of trees. Near the Texas-Louisiana border close to Tyler, he could easily see himself getting lost and finally finding some peace until time to go to trial.

So why was his first thought that he didn't want to disappoint the blue-eyed, ponytail-wearing marshal sitting out front?

Chapter Two

Five minutes blew by too fast. She had a few more to give. Eight minutes ticked by with no Brewer. She'd lost her witness. The man had probably opened a bathroom window and escaped out the back like in the movies. *Great.* She checked the clock again and tapped her finger on the steering wheel. Nine minutes. Time to call it in. Crystal reached for her cell as the door to the café opened. Out came Brewer. He strolled to the passenger side, casual as anyone pleased before opening the door and claiming the seat.

"Let's do this," he said causally, like she hadn't been sitting here sweating bullets the entire time he'd been gone.

"Good." As she put the gearshift in Reverse, her cell buzzed. "Do you mind if I get that?" She checked the screen and then flashed eyes at him. "Family emergency."

"Be my guest." He glanced around and then unbuckled. "Should I drive?"

Crystal shook her head and refrained from calling him out for being irritating. After pulling over to the side of the parking lot, she answered her sister's call. "Everything okay, Abi?"

The line was quiet, which sent Crystal's stress levels soaring.

"Abi?"

"Hi, yes, everything's fine now, considering the circumstances." Abi cleared her throat like she did when she was hiding the fact she'd been crying.

Abilene Remington was not a crier. Despite being five years younger, she could hold her own in a fight too. The fact that she'd been crying triggered alarms inside Crystal's head. "Did something else happen this morning?"

"Gram coded," Abi supplied before quickly adding, "but her heart is beating again."

Crystal frowned as a moment of panic seized her. Holding back the swell of emotions gathering in her chest like a storm, she muttered a stream of curse words. "Oh, Abi. That's not good. Are you there right now?"

"No," Abi admitted. "I had to leave. Which makes everything so much worse, right?"

Yes, it did. The imagination ran wild when a loved one was sick or in the hospital and you couldn't be there to see how the person looked, breathed, rested with your own eyes, or to ask the doctor questions when you caught her or him in the hall. Gauging someone's reactions on a screen only went so far. It was better than nothing, but there was no replacement for being physically present.

Crystal and Abi were in the same boat as far as not being at the hospital. Her siblings and cousins were also US marshals. They couldn't all leave the job at the same time with their caseloads, so they'd worked out a system. Her brother, Duke, had been able to arrange to come back to the ranch first, then Crystal hoped it would be her turn. A selfish part of her wished Brewer had disappeared out that bathroom window a few minutes ago so she could head to Mesa Point. "This setback will complicate her recovery, won't it?"

"I thought we were going to lose her, Crys." Abi rarely called Crystal that name. "And Duke was back at the ranch with Nash." Shiloh Nash was the ranch foreman.

Pinching the bridge of her nose with her free hand, she exhaled. "I'm sorry you had to be alone at the hospital when that happened." Crystal had been assigned to pick up Brewer, which also wasn't going as planned. "That's my fault, and I—"

"Work happens," Abi interrupted. "We all agreed to this. You couldn't have known what would happen. Besides, everything was stable four hours ago. Being here is essentially like watching paint dry until it isn't."

"I'm still sorry that I wasn't there, Abs." Another rarely used pet name they'd developed joking around with each other after Krav Maga class. Hitting Abi in the abs had been like slamming a fist into steel.

She glanced over at Brewer, who was pretending to check his cell phone instead of listening. Why did that worry her? "This assignment might wrap up sooner than I originally believed, so I might be back before you know it."

"Camden can take a few days off." Their cousin was the oldest of the six. Crystal was second oldest. "Said he'll be here after he files papers on his last assignment." Abi paused. "It's just hard sometimes, you know?"

"I do," Crystal reassured. "Our grandparents are lucky to have you there to make sure they have everything they need."

"Just wish they would wake up. Then again, while I'm wishing, I may as well wish this was all a bad dream."

"Words can't express how much we all want that to happen."

Their condition after a near-fatal car crash had been stable over the past few days, but Dr. Abel had warned anything could happen. Their advanced ages weren't helping matters, and the doctor had no guesses as to how long the two might be in a coma. The only comforting thought was that the two of them were going through it together. They functioned like hydrogen and oxygen, and one wouldn't be able to breathe without the other. The fact that Duke had arranged to have them moved into the same room provided a small measure of comfort in a dire situation.

"Let me know when Camden gets there. Okay?" she said.

"I will." Abi's word was as good as gold. "You have to go, don't you?"

"I'm sorry," Crystal said for the third time. She'd say it a thousand more if it meant their grandparents would wake up.

"It's fine," her sister reassured, even though it wasn't. It might never be fine again if they lost Lorenzo and Lacy Remington, and they both knew it. "Call me later if you want to talk."

Crystal promised she would before saying goodbye and ending the call. Without another word, she put the gearshift in Drive and navigated onto I-45. Normally, she wouldn't allow her personal life to interfere while on an assignment, but this was life-or-death and she couldn't perform her job to the best of her ability without staying plugged into what was happening in Mesa Point.

For the next couple of hours, Brewer tilted the seat back and closed his eyes for the ride while Crystal ruminated about the accident that had left her grandparents fighting for their lives. She should have been the one on the back road leading to their property instead of them. She should have been the one to find them after the accident instead of Audrey Newcastle, soon to be Remington, but that was hardly the point. And she should have been the one sitting in the blue chair on top of nondescript blue carpet in a blue waiting room when her beloved grandmother had coded instead of out here negotiating with someone who figured they could save their own life better than she could protect it.

Halfway to Dallas, Brewer stirred. He sat up and hit the button to make the seat back rise. His intense gaze fixed out the front windshield. She hadn't intended for him to know anything about her personal life while on the job. It was the reason most US marshals she knew didn't wear a wedding ring or have screen savers of their husbands, wives, or children. Not that she had any of those things. Still. That wasn't the point. The less others knew, the better. This situation couldn't be helped. He needed to know that she might have to check in or take calls from home but she had no intention of abandoning him.

"There's something going on with my family that won't affect my job," she said.

He didn't respond.

"I just thought you should know I'm dedicated to your safety until I see this through no matter how long it takes." Work came first. It had always come first. Nature of the job. "And I will need to take a personal call from time to time." She prayed not one with bad news. "But if you're uncomfortable with this arrangement, I can call my supervisor, get myself replaced." It would take time. It would take some shuffling. But she might be able to pull it off.

Nothing.

BREWER DIDN'T HAVE the heart to be a jerk to Crystal after overhearing her side of the phone call. "I don't have an issue, ma'am." He figured once they got to Dallas and settled in, he'd find a way to ditch her and get to Trent's location off the grid anyway. Brewer had no idea what he'd find once he got there, and that suited him just fine. Could be nothing more than a campsite. But he needed to figure out transportation since he'd left his vehicle with his aunt in case she needed it.

Either way, he'd make do.

"Okay," she said. "You can call me Crystal. Every time I hear *ma'am* or *Ms. Remington*, I check over the shoulder for my grandmother." Her voice hitched on the last word.

Was it his place to say anything?

Why the hell not. "I'm sorry to hear about your family situation, ma'am… Crystal." Calling her by her first name would take some getting used to.

"Thank you." Those two words were spoken with genuine appreciation. Brewer had become good at reading people after being in charge of interrogations for a stint. He'd learned to listen for subtle clues. For instance, liars usually spoke slower, paused for longer periods, and spoke with a higher pitch. Crystal's voice filled with warmth rather than her usual straight-to-the-point tone. "My grandparents have always been the rock of our family, so it's unnatural for them to be so…helpless."

"What about your folks, if you don't mind my asking."

"Gone." The word came out so easily that whatever had happened must have been a long time ago. "I have two siblings and three cousins, but we're all like siblings because we grew up together. My father abandoned us after Abi was born."

"I'm sorry."

"Thank you," she said, keeping her eyes forward on the stretch of road in front of them.

"Your mother?" he asked.

"Died during childbirth with Abi." Some of the tension eased as she relaxed into her seat. "I'm the oldest, and my brother, Duke, is in the middle."

"It must have been hard growing up without a mother." He should know.

"We had our grandparents. That made a huge difference in our lives. In fact, I'm not sure where any of us would have ended up without them." She tapped the steering wheel with her right thumb. A nervous habit? "They raised us and our three cousins who, by the way, now all work as US marshals, same as our grandfather did once."

He made a face. "That's odd, isn't it?"

"We're not that much different than military families," she stated. "Our grandfather started off his career as a US marshal but left as soon as he saved enough money to start his paint-horse ranch. He couldn't stand being away from our grandmother for even a few days."

"Makes sense." Brewer understood military often ran in families but couldn't relate to being in the kind of relationship with someone that would make him want to overhaul his life so they could spend more time together. It boggled the mind.

"What happened to your aunt and uncle?" he asked.

His aunt had been his lifeline and probably the one person in Galveston who didn't have a bone to pick with him from something he'd done during his time there. Getting her out of harm's way had been his first priority when he'd learned Crane's arrest had gone down. Aunt Rosemary had taken him in when no one else would. She'd never once turned her back, no matter how much he'd deserved it. He owed her.

"My aunt took off a few months after my cousin Dalton was born, we still don't know why," she informed. "My uncle died when we were all young. And then there's my own father who split after my mother died."

"Sounds like a real jerk."

"Agreed," she said with authority. "He's remarried with a new family and no time for the old one. Although, my brother said our dad called recently, probably sniffing around to see if there was an inheritance in the near future."

Exactly the reason Brewer had no plans to tie the knot with anyone. Marriage was antiquated. The idea had had its day. Long-term commitment had proven to be impossible and overrated. His own parents were all the proof he needed.

Brewer glanced down to where his left shin used to be. Underneath his cargo pants, it was impossible to see the prosthetic leg. He knew part of himself was missing now and would never be replaced no matter how many advances were made in medicine. No one would want to spend the rest of their life with a partial man.

"I've been going on and on about my family. I'm not usually this talkative. I apologize." Crystal blushed, and it only served to make her more attractive.

"Don't," he said. "It's making the time pass faster, and I'm interested in hearing more. Takes my mind off my current problems."

"It's just not what I do when I'm working. Better to keep a hard line between personal and professional. I hope you can understand."

He leaned his head back. "Do I ever. The only way to survive in the military is to push all thoughts other than survival out of your mind. Right before a mission, I used to take a few minutes to think about what I'd be doing once it was over. Plant the seed that I was confident that no matter what I faced that day, I'd be back in a few hours, days, or weeks, playing a pickup game with one of the guys in my unit after chow time."

"Sounds like a good strategy."

"It kept me alive this long," he mused. Even though he hadn't exactly come home whole. "Other than Aunt Rosemary, I didn't have anyone else to come home to like some of the men. They'd stare at a picture of their girlfriend or wife. Some had kids. They would memorize those smiling faces and take that into a combat zone with them. It was enough to assure they came out alive."

"It's good to have something or someone to look forward to."

She had to have read in his file there was no one in his life. "What about you? Anyone special you're going home to?"

He half expected her to remind him that her personal life was none of his business. Instead, she shocked him by saying, "Not in a long time."

A beautiful, intelligent woman like her shouldn't have to be alone. "Too busy?"

She opened her mouth to speak before clamping it shut again. He'd crossed a line he shouldn't have.

"Sorry," he said. "You don't have to answer that. I get it. Your personal life is on a need-to-know basis, and I don't need to know."

"Something like that."

"I'm just killing time." He checked the burner cell. Two people had the number, Aunt Rosemary and now Trent. "Didn't mean to step out of bounds with my questions." He was more curious about Crystal Remington's life than he had a right to be. He wanted to know what brimmed under the surface of that serious facade. Did she have a sense of humor to go with her determination and intelligence?

"If we're going to spend twenty-four seven together over the next couple of days until the hearing, it might not hurt to get to know each other better," she said. "Relationship status is the only topic out of bounds, as you said."

He didn't feel good lying about his plans to ditch her and head toward Tyler. But what could he do?

"A name came up in the investigation into your case. Who is Damon O'Meara?"

"Damon the Devil?" he asked.

"Sure," she said. "I guess that's the same one."

"He's been showing up with the Lithuanian lately," Brewer said.

"Who is the Lithuanian?" she asked.

Brewer shrugged. "You got me. That's the only name I ever heard him called by. I think he's close to Victor Crane. A confidant or right hand. He didn't interact with me. I only ever managed to see him from behind."

"Interesting," she noted.

That was all he had about the Lithuanian, so he steered the conversation back to personal life. "You were telling me about your family. Was there some kind of accident that caused your grandparents to be in the hospital?"

"Car crash," she answered. "Did you know that in Texas there's at least one traffic fatality every day?"

"I didn't, but after growing up driving on country roads I'm not exactly shocked."

Crystal nodded. "My grandfather is getting older." She gripped the wheel tighter. He noticed she did this every time she spoke about her grandparents or the accident. "He's too stubborn to give up his driver's license no matter how many times we try to ease into the subject."

"A person like him would fiercely guard his independence, I'm guessing."

"Yes, and I get it on some level."

"Aunt Rosemary refuses to drive over thirty-five miles an hour no matter what the speed limit is." Brewer's biggest fear was that she would cause an accident. "She knows better than to go out at night, though. Her eyes aren't what they used to be."

"Does she still drive?"

"Only if it's an emergency," he said. "For the most part, I finally got her to give up her keys."

"How on earth did you do that?"

He shook his head and cracked a smile. "It won't work with your grandfather."

"How do you know?"

"Trust me."

"That's a two-way street," she quipped, full of sass and vinegar. "That trust thing. Why not trust me enough to tell me in case it could help me figure out how to keep my grandfather from ever driving again once this is over?"

"Because I seriously doubt the man wants hot firemen, as my aunt puts it, driving him to run errands or to take his wife to a doctor's appointment."

"You hired off-duty firemen to drive your aunt?" she asked with what sounded like a whole new respect for him and more than a little admiration.

"Damn right I did."

The fact she cracked a smile shouldn't cause his heart to squeeze. But it did.

Chapter Three

Crystal cracked a smile. "Sexy firemen definitely won't work with my grandfather. Brilliant idea, though." She had to give that one to him.

"What can I say? Aunt Rosemary got a kick out of it, and it got her off the road." From the sound of his voice, he was smiling too. Why did that strike her as a rare occurrence? More importantly, why did it warm her heart so much?

Based on Brewer's current situation, he hadn't had a whole lot to be happy about lately either. She'd read in his file that he'd lost part of his leg before being offered medical retirement from the military. She knew he'd refused psych help, saying he would take care of it on his own. And now he'd learned he was working for a crime-ring leader.

To say he'd been through a lot lately was like saying Texas summers were brutal. Yes, they were. End of story.

As strange as it probably sounded, even to her, she liked opening up to Brewer and talking about her family. The reason was probably more related to all the pressure she'd been under and not that there was chemistry between them. Reading too much into it would be a mistake. He was a captive audience, and she needed to get a few things off her chest. Normally, she would talk to her grandmother if something was eating at her. Since that wasn't an option, Brewer was the closest person in proximity and didn't seem to mind.

When he spoke, he had the kind of honest, direct voice that put her at ease. Too much so?

It also wrapped her in warmth and created all kinds of sensations in her body best ignored and forgotten. She'd never experienced sensations like those simply from the sound of someone's voice.

Crystal reminded herself not to get too attached. This assignment would be over in a matter of days, a week tops since the district attorney was trying to push through a speedy trial date. The case against Crane was cut-and-dried, and a witness was at risk. Judges tended to be more accommodating under those circumstances. Court dates magically opened up while other cases languished.

It was good this would be over soon. She needed to get to the hospital in Mesa Point.

GPS let them know the turnoff was one mile ahead. I-45 turned into North Central Expressway. They had a town house waiting for them in University Park, a ritzy area just north of Dallas. It had been finagled by Crystal's supervisor, who'd told her not to get used to living in the lap of luxury. She didn't see how that was possible considering the family horse ranch in Mesa Point was enough to keep anyone's feet on the ground. Not to mention a marshal's salary wasn't exactly putting her in the top one percent. The paint-horse ranch barely made ends meet, but the home and land were paid for and it had provided for six kids while keeping her grandparents fed and happy. They'd always intended to divide the ranch equally among all six of the grandkids. Crystal couldn't begin to think about a day when her grandparents didn't live there and work the business they'd built together after Grandpa Lor's stint as a marshal.

"It'll be good to get in and get settled before it gets too late." She was still surprised Brewer had come out of the restaurant when she'd been about to call it in. He'd taken his sweet time in exiting, though, which said he'd probably been in the bathroom thinking seriously about his options. "We'll have to stay indoors once we arrive, but I think you'll find the place easy on the eyes. We don't normally get such a swanky safe house."

"Don't I feel special?" He'd shifted gears and was now staring out the passenger window in quiet contemplation. Why did she get the sinking feeling he was considering ditching her?

She blew it off as a combination of stress and nerves.

"Your file gave me information about the situation you're currently in," she started, changing the subject, and turning the tables. "What made you go into the military?"

"My high school guidance counselor said I had a lot of anger." He surprised her in talking about his past. "Tried to get me to join the football team."

"I'm guessing you said no."

"Organized sports were never going to be my thing." He rubbed the strap of his backpack in between this thumb and forefinger. "Plus, I wouldn't have known when to stop if someone came at me hotheaded. It would have gotten ugly fast."

"What did you do instead?" she asked. "To get out your anger."

"Got suspended mostly." He chuckled. "I'm not exactly proud of some of the things I did when I had too much testosterone and not enough common sense. I read somewhere once that the decision-making filter in the front of the teen brain takes a break for a couple of years. I got out of hand a few too many times, but never unprovoked. I'm not saying that makes it right, but I didn't start fights. Not even then. Although, looking back, I can admit to overreacting too much of the time."

"What made you so angry?"

"The usual predictable stuff," he continued. "Had a drunk for a dad who used to beat the hell out of me for no reason except sometimes I breathed too loudly. A mom who couldn't take living with an abusive husband, so she bolted without looking back, saving herself and leaving me with a monster."

"You didn't tell anyone about the abuse?"

He shook his head without missing a beat. "Ever hear the saying about the devil you know being better than the one you don't? It's the reason most kids don't turn their parents in. They have no idea what will happen to them if they do."

"Did your aunt step in at some point?" Crystal asked. "Is that why you take such good care of her?"

"Yes, ma—" He stopped himself. "Yes, she did. She's an angel in my book. She started off asking my father if I could come to her house after school. Then, she would come up with an excuse to keep me later, like I wasn't done with my homework. Once eight o'clock hit, he'd been too drunk to care where the hell his son was. If she could keep me until then, we were home free. I spent most nights there and then weekends with him until she had me living with her full-time by sophomore year. No matter how bad I was, she saw a piece of good in me." He shrugged. "I'll never understand it because I sure as hell didn't deserve or appreciate her enough at the time."

"The world needs more Aunt Rosemarys." She would add her grandparents Lorenzo and Lacy to the list too. It amazed her that they'd taken on six kids who were within seven years of each other. The teenage years had seen a whole lot of doors slamming and arguments that had needed interventions. The Remingtons had been good kids, but no one would call them angels. Those angsty temperamental teenage years had left no prisoners. "And grandparents like mine."

"I'll second that," he concurred. "Your grandparents must have had their hands full with all... How many did you say there were of you in total?"

"Six," she answered. "I was just calculating our ages in my head. We're all within a seven-year span. Working from the youngest to oldest, Dalton and Abi are the same age. They're both twenty-eight years old. They were close growing up since they were in the same grade. Then there's my brother, Duke, who's thirty now. He just got engaged. Jules is thirty-two. Her real name is Julie. I'm thirty-three." She shot major side-eye at him. "Don't you dare say anything about me getting old."

He put his hands up, palms out, in the surrender position. "Wasn't planning on doing anything of the kind."

"Good. That leaves my cousin Camden, who's thirty-five."

"Which also makes you the second oldest, if my calculations are correct." He put his hands down and returned to working the strap of his backpack between his thumb and forefinger.

"That's right," she agreed, pulling into the parking lot of the town house. After finding a parking spot away from the street, she texted her contact to let him know they'd arrived. The response came a few seconds later. "He's on his way. Should take about fifteen to twenty minutes."

Brewer leaned his seat back again. "Guess we have time to get comfortable, then."

She wasn't touching that statement with a ten-foot pole. There was never a moment in this job where she felt like she could ever relax. After work? Sure. Never during work hours. She cut off the engine. "You were telling me about your family."

The look he shot almost made her laugh. Turned out the intense former military sergeant had a sense of humor.

"Nice try, Crystal." The way her name rolled off his tongue shouldn't have sent goose bumps across sensitized skin. He had one of those voices that she was certain had seduced every woman he'd set his sights on.

It wouldn't work on this one, all sense of professionalism and code of conduct aside. A man like Brewer was dangerous. She had no doubt he had a *take no prisoners* approach to love.

Love? Since when did she begin thinking about the love life of those in her charge?

This wasn't the time to start.

BREWER NEVER HAD a problem cutting bait and moving on in any situation he'd been in, until now. He tucked his cell inside the pocket of his rucksack, secure in the knowledge he had the coordinates safely in his phone for when he needed them. There was a wad of cash inside a zippered pocket. It was enough to get him through a couple of weeks if he needed that long, which he didn't expect to. Still, survival took planning.

Leaving Crystal wasn't something he wanted to do so

much as needed to at this point. Depending on others hadn't proven to be the best plan. Staying meant being responsible for her life in addition to his own. Although she wouldn't see it that way.

Brewer knew the kind of man he was up against. He knew who the lieutenants she'd mentioned were. Hell, he'd driven his boss—someone he'd believed to be a successful businessman when he'd taken the gig while fresh out of the military—to meetings with those men. Brewer could name all of them. He wished his word could put them all behind bars, but the DA had said he could only prove an association if Brewer had witnessed a crime. Overhearing information about a crime was circumstantial evidence and wouldn't hold up in court.

With his background, he was probably lucky the DA hadn't locked him up in the same cell as Crane. But then, Brewer had gone to the district attorney's office with proof of a crime. He'd witnessed Crane order a hit. Better yet, he'd recorded the meeting once he'd realized what was happening.

As a driver, Brewer had built trust with Crane based on his background and military experience. Trent had vouched for Brewer, so there'd been no reason for distrust. He certainly wasn't a plant from the government. In fact, he was still angry about the bad intelligence his superior officer had acted on that had cost two of his friends' lives, part of his leg, and hearing out of his right ear.

The explosion, the losses, still haunted his dreams.

He'd known the job he'd been signing up for in the military. In many ways, going into the service had saved his life. It had certainly changed his perspective and the man he'd become. Given him honor and a reason to hold his head up high.

Didn't mean he would do a few critical things over if he could go back in time. It should have been him driving the Humvee that day, not Randal. It should have been him who'd had to be pieced back together to ship his body home after the IED had blown up. And it should have been him who'd come home in a box.

Randal had volunteered to drive that sweltering day. He'd argued it was his turn even though everyone had known it was Brewer's. Thanks to a raging headache, Brewer had gladly turned over the keys. Beer pong out of boredom the night before had cost a man's life. Brewer had gone to the back of the Humvee to lie down and cover his eyes from the unforgiving sunlight while they'd driven on their mission. Only two of the four had returned to camp alive.

Brewer didn't care about Crane's men coming after him. He only had to live long enough to ensure the bastard spent the rest of his life behind bars. The men were ruthless and would show no mercy in the event they found Brewer first. He had news for them—they weren't the first ones who'd tried to kill him. Knowing his luck, they wouldn't be the last.

"You got quiet on me." Crystal's voice pulled him from his deep thoughts.

He shook his head like he could somehow shake off his frustration at coming home to Texas a broken man who was now a witness, tricked into working for a bad man. "What do you want to talk about while we wait? Or should we get out of this car and stretch our legs?"

"It's probably not a good idea to be seen, unless you have a cramp you need to work out." She glanced over and then immediately returned her gaze to the patch of wind-shield directly in front of her. Was she curious about what the prosthetic looked like?

Brewer wasn't in the mood to talk about it or what had happened to cause the injury.

The woman was intelligent and beautiful. He'd rather learn more about her. "I get that your job runs in the family, but why did you decide a career as a marshal was the right job for you?" he asked.

"Why do you question it? Because I'm a woman?" She'd mentioned that before, and he honestly didn't care one way or the other.

"No," he said, deciding not to go down the road of explaining his viewpoint a second time when the first apparently hadn't taken. "Of all the jobs in the world, why this one? You grew up on a horse ranch. I see why your grandfather started in law enforcement and then moved to the country for peace. The other way around doesn't make as much sense to me. This doesn't seem like the logical next step."

"I guess not," she conceded, rubbing her temples. She'd been through hell with the accident. It was easy to see how much she loved her grandparents.

The only way he could relate was because of Aunt Rosemary. She'd been the first person to stick up for him and tell him that he was better than his actions. It might have taken a bit for him to believe it too, but he'd finally gotten there.

"The respect I have for my grandfather set the stage for me and the others to follow in his footsteps," she said. "But you're right. Every law enforcement officer I know has a story as to why they decided on this job."

"Do you?" It was probably not the best question. "I'm guessing so."

"Stick around and I might tell you mine."

"What's that supposed to mean?" he asked. She couldn't possibly have read his mind.

A navy blue Tahoe pulled into the parking lot and parked two spaces away.

"Save it for later?" she asked with a wink. The move was most definitely not flirtatious. It was more like *I've got your number.*

Had she figured out that he planned to disappear after she went to sleep? How? It wasn't like she had a crystal ball or mind-reading capabilities. Was she that good at reading people? At reading him?

A man in his late forties who looked dressed for the golf course stepped out of the Tahoe.

Crystal exited the driver's side of her sedan. Before closing the door, she said, "I'll be right back."

The exchange took less than three minutes, according to Brewer's watch—a watch he never went anywhere without.

After the driver returned to his seat and the Tahoe pulled out of his spot, Crystal motioned for Brewer to join her. She walked to the back of her vehicle and popped open the trunk before retrieving an overnight bag. She'd done this before. Many times if he had to guess.

When he left tonight, he'd tape a note to explain himself on the fridge. He owed her that much after she'd talked to him on a personal level. It was the right thing to do.

A quick tour of the two-story town house convinced Brewer this was probably the fanciest place he would ever stay in. It was tempting to stick around for the primary suite alone, which had a bathtub the size of a two-person hot tub. The mental image of Crystal joining him in there naked needed to go.

After setting his rucksack down in that room, once Crystal had made it clear she wouldn't have it any other way, he joined her in the living room.

"Are you hungry?" she asked, picking up the TV's remote.

"I could eat." Brewer could go without food longer than most. But there was nothing to do except kill time, so he might as well go along with the idea.

A moment later, Crystal's expression twisted to fierce determination as she dived toward him, knocking him off his feet. The move surprised him because she knew exactly where to aim to knock him off balance—not an easy thing to do.

The hearing loss in his right ear made him miss the sound of the shot until the bullet had pierced the front window, which was a few seconds too late.

Chapter Four

"Stay down," Crystal said to Brewer, cursing the fact their safe house had been compromised.

It was unlikely they'd been followed but not impossible.

Dealing with a high-level long-standing criminal operation raised the stakes. She was good at her job, but so were they. And they didn't get to be one of the top crime organizations in Texas by being sloppy or allowing witnesses to make it to trial to testify.

Despite keeping vigilant watch, she couldn't be one hundred percent positive she hadn't picked up a tail. *Dammit.*

Was she too distracted by her family crisis to do a good job?

Diving on top of Brewer had been instinct. In that split second, reason hadn't kicked in to tell her that he used to be military and could handle himself. Brewer rolled out from underneath her in one swift move. It happened so fast she landed on the hardwood flooring with a thud.

"They'll expect us to come out the back door," she said, belly crawling away from the kitchen. The town house had a typical shotgun layout with a bathroom to the right.

"Bathroom?" he asked. He must have already memorized the layout. She should have known he would get the lay of the land in a matter of minutes. She did the same.

Memorizing exits was the curse, or blessing, depending on how you looked at it, of working in a job that could get you killed on a daily basis.

"Yes," she said. She'd already pulled her Glock from her shoulder harness and was army crawling while holding her weapon out in front of her.

Brewer managed to gather and then slip his rucksack onto his back without missing a beat. His clear thinking and presence of mind wasn't something she was used to in a witness. Protecting a former Army sergeant was virgin territory. The guy could hold his own, but she had better resources at her disposal—resources that he was going to need to stay alive and make it to trial.

At this point, Crystal was following Brewer's lead. He navigated them to the bathroom. The window next to the toilet was shaped like a cruise ship's. Could Brewer fit through the octagon shape?

"Here, let me," she said.

He spun around until he was back-to-back with her as she stood up and took a peek out. She lifted her head barely enough to survey the area. A man wearing all dark clothing moved around the side of the town house. He was carrying, and she suspected his target practice was decent if he'd been selected for this job.

A long-range shot would make for quick and easy witness removal. No one would even get their hands dirty handling "the problem" in that manner.

Crystal got a good look at the shooter's profile. A bounty hunter? Protecting Brewer just got a whole lot trickier.

"There's a bounty on your head," she whispered to him, just in case he decided to get cute and ditch her in the chaos that was bound to follow.

Brewer muttered the same curse she was thinking.

"You're a high-value target," she said to him as the bounty hunter rounded the back of the town house. "And I have a feeling this guy is about to come in through the back door in a matter of a few seconds, so we'd better get the hell out of here if we both want to stay alive."

Brewer moved to open the window. "You want out first?"

The sound of the back door being kicked in echoed through the home.

Without saying a word, Crystal climbed out the window and then landed hard on prickly shrubbery that wrapped its arms around her. She bucked before rolling onto the hard soil. A few scratches never killed anyone.

Once again, she was left holding her breath to see if Brewer would follow. Had she made a mistake in going first? She couldn't exactly call out to him.

The thought that he might be in trouble stopped her cold as she stared at the small window.

"Dammit," he said with a grunt. His voice traveled out the window into the still night air.

Crystal couldn't climb back in the way she'd gotten out, so she bolted around to the back door and then into the kitchen. The bounty hunter had kicked the door in, just like she'd suspected. At this point, she assumed he worked alone, like most in his profession. Profit sharing wasn't exactly a common business practice.

Bounty hunters were the lone rangers of the twenty-first century. They weren't bound by laws like marshals and others who worked in law enforcement. They weren't above them either. In general, they were end of the line, the last resort in trying to locate someone. Did Cane's men want Brewer alive? Did they want to mete out their own form of justice?

A thud shook the walls of the town house. Crystal turned off lights as she carefully, methodically moved through the town house.

A series of grunts and curses twisted her stomach in knots. From this vantage point, she had no idea if Brewer was winning the fight.

At least no weapons had been fired, which was part of the reason she believed this might be a "bring 'em back alive" order. Proof of death would be easy enough if the bounty hunter shot Brewer and then took a photo.

Photos could be doctored, but even the most dishonest person would realize sending in a fake would cost their own life when dealing with someone like Crane.

A bounty made a difficult protection detail a dozen times harder. If they weren't so short-staffed at the marshal's office already, she would request help. Several marshals had turned in their badges, saying the public didn't appreciate their service any longer so they didn't see the need to put their lives on the line.

If being a US marshal wasn't in her blood, she might feel the same way.

Another crash sounded, tightening the knot. She took another step toward the bathroom. At least she had on her Kevlar vest underneath her suit jacket.

The light flipped off in the bathroom, casting the place in darkness. There was a little light from the street streaming in between the mini-blind slats. It was enough.

As she approached the bathroom, a body came flying out.

"Put your hands where I can see 'em," she demanded the second she realized it was the bounty hunter and not Brewer.

He appeared next, taking up the door frame before launching himself toward the bounty hunter. You'd think both had just run a marathon for their heavy breathing.

In the next second, Brewer had the bounty hunter pinned to the floor with his knee jammed into the guy's back. "Who sent you?"

The bounty hunter turned his face to the side and grinned.

The question had to be asked, even though she would have been more surprised if he'd answered.

"It's your death sentence," Crystal said, keeping a watchful eye on the doors. "Are you by yourself, or should I break out the charcuterie board for company?"

The bounty hunter chuckled at her sarcasm, then winced when Brewer ground his knee harder into the man's back.

"What's your name?" she asked, moving toward him to relieve him of his wallet so she could retrieve his ID. Folks in this line of work didn't always carry identification in the event that, well, something just like this happened and they got caught on the wrong side of the law. Checking pockets was still mandatory.

Still no word from the bounty hunter.

"Cat got your tongue?" she goaded. On occasion, one of the folks' ego swelled when she poked the bear so to speak. Most weren't exactly reading Shakespeare in their time off. Muscle people like this one rarely read much more than texts with names of their targets and the price on their head. Speaking of texts, she searched him for his phone.

This guy was shrewd based on the fact he'd left any identifiers either in his vehicle or at home. He didn't have a cell on him, which was rare, but she'd come across his type in her line of work.

Only an experienced bounty hunter would take a job like

this one. If a hunter left any ties leading back to the organization, they would be erased. Crane ran a tight ship—one that had escaped the scrutiny of law enforcement for the past seven years. Well, guess what? Time was up.

BREWER FINALLY CAUGHT his breath as Crystal heaved a sigh. Being dramatic must've been part of playing a role.

In battle, there were rules that had to be followed. Brewer figured home was no different. As much as those rules got in the way of forcing someone to speak, they were as much the reason he took pride in his military service as backyard barbecues and families huddled around shiny trees on Christmas morning. For better or worse, rules protected people. He'd had a bird's-eye view of countries without order. Chaos. It gave him a new appreciation for home. That and the fact bullets weren't flying over his head every five minutes.

"Talk, sonofabitch," Brewer managed to grind out the words.

"It's all good," Crystal said to him. "Dallas PD will have a good time arresting this one." With that, she pulled out her cell phone and called 911. She walked away before she identified herself to Dispatch.

The bounty hunter Brewer had pinned to the floor was trying to kill him and not her. Although this jerk didn't look like he would mind a little collateral damage.

The man was half a foot shorter than Brewer, so five feet, ten inches of a tank of a man. The guy bleached the top of his short, spiky hair, leaving the sides black. Brewer had stared into the eyes of folks with no souls. Folks who would use women or children without a thought as a means to an end, strapping a bomb to them and sending them into enemy camp. Evil always showed through the eyes.

This sonofabitch had no conscience and was greedy. He hadn't shot Brewer when he'd had the chance, so the bounty must've been to bring him in. Brewer didn't have to be one of them to realize what that meant. Torture. Make an example out of him in case anyone else in the organization grew a conscience and decided to testify against the boss. Or if the feds had put pressure on some of the "employees" of the organization, had anyone close to turning state's witness.

People needed a leader. Some might view Brewer's actions as leadership. They might be tempted to follow suit.

Crane would want to squash that instinct like a cockroach.

The bounty hunter tried to buck Brewer off to no avail. He might have gotten in a few good punches, but Brewer was strong as an ox and about as heavy as one too. Going to the gym, pushing himself to the limit with endless burpees that he hated doing and pull-ups along with weights and about a dozen other exercises made all the body parts he had left strong.

Within a matter of minutes after the call, the town house was flooded with law enforcement officers. After exchanging what looked like a coin with the lead officer on the scene, Crystal turned to him. "We need to talk."

With the bounty hunter under arrest, Brewer could finally catch his breath, think about his next step. "Okay."

She walked into the kitchen area where a handyman had just arrived to fix the back door.

"I understand if you don't trust my ability to keep you safe, but—"

"Whoa," Brewer said, interrupting her. "What gives you that impression?"

Crystal-blue eyes studied him as she folded her arms

across her chest. "The safe house was compromised minutes after we arrived." She shrugged. "I figured after almost getting ditched back at the diner that you'd definitely want to be rid of me now."

"I'm alive because of your quick thinking," he corrected. He knew a good teammate when he encountered one. He brought his hand up to his right ear. "I'm sure you've read my file. I can't hear out of this side. It's the reason I never heard the bullet. If you hadn't jumped me, I would likely be dead right now. If anything, this has shown me that I do need someone else to have my back."

Crystal was good at her job. She'd proven her abilities. They made a good team. And a growing part of him didn't want to let her down in return. Could he take her off the grid with him? Would she agree?

Chapter Five

"First of all," Crystal shot back, appreciating the first break in tension and show of trust in her abilities since meeting Brewer this morning, "I didn't 'jump' you." She flashed eyes at him. "You'd know it if I did."

Her sarcasm brought out a smirk. It wasn't exactly another smile, but she could work with it. The fact that the mood could lighten so quickly after what had just happened told her that he'd been one damn fine sergeant. He was used to bullets and battle. After seeing him in action, she was a little less offended that he'd tried to cut her out of the equation. The man was capable of taking care of himself.

Still, she had resources available that he didn't. It gave her an edge, and he'd finally conceded as much. She could exhale now despite the fact her heart pounded at the thought of spending time alone with Wade Brewer.

She shoved the unprofessional reaction out of her thoughts.

"This bastard is facing a third-degree-felony charge," she said to Brewer to get the conversation going again.

"Think there's a snowball's chance in hell that he'll talk?" he asked, leaning a slender hip against the counter. The sleeve of his shirt was ripped, displaying a peek of a tattoo on his bicep. The man's arms were thick, tan, and muscled. She had a thing for men with well-placed tattoos despite her squeaky-clean image and the fact she had none of her own. The right one could be sexy as all get-out. Too many and it came across as a doodling on someone's body. Most of the time, it looked like a hot mess.

Brewer's fit into the *sexy* category from what she could see.

Good for him. He probably had no trouble dating, whereas Crystal had been in a drought of her own doing. Ever since her breakup with Lucas Mahone, she'd been content to spend Saturday nights at home with a good book and a glass of wine when she wasn't on the job. Lucas had been "the one" on paper. He was good looking. Was a solid marshal who worked a different district than hers, despite putting in a bid to transfer. Never been married. No kids. Not that she minded either, but he wasn't hung up on the past or tied to someone he didn't want to be with any longer.

And yet dating him felt a lot like drinking milk. Plain. Probably even good for you. Last Christmas, though, he'd given her a new seat for her bicycle. Had she needed one? Yes. Did it make riding her bicycle more comfortable? Yes. Was it practical? Yes.

Therein lies the problem. He was a practical choice. He was comfortable. He was measured.

Did he make her palms sweaty? No.

Did he make her stomach flip-flop? No.

Did he make her skin sizzle with his touch? Absolutely not.

So, she'd done the only kind thing she could think of. Rather than draw out the relationship another few months or, worse yet, years, she'd cut him loose so he could find someone who would be a better match.

Lucas had another trait. This one had become annoying. He was stubborn, said he'd win her back. Six months later, he was doubling down despite her best efforts to handle the breakup in a professional manner.

Crystal had learned a valuable lesson through this experience—never date anyone even remotely connected to her job.

To make matters worse, Lucas's transfer had been approved since they were so short-staffed in her district. He'd made the move last week.

"Hey," Brewer said, snapping his fingers in front of her eyes. "Anybody home?"

"Yes, sorry," she said, giving herself a mental headshake. "Did you say something?"

He studied her a little more intensely now. "I have a place where we can go off the grid."

"I have to be in contact with my supervisor at all times," she said, shaking her head. Brewer might've been fully capable of taking care of himself, but she couldn't let him take over. "In fact, she's coming up with a new plan for us right now."

"Excuse me for saying but this one didn't exactly work out," he said, twisting his face in disdain. "To be clear, you're good at what you do, but my trust in the process ends there."

She couldn't argue his point even though she wanted to.

"I have a certain protocol to follow, Brewer." She shrugged. "If you want me, you'll have to go along with it." Her cheeks flamed. "I didn't mean *want* me." Words came out all wrong when she got flustered.

The freakin' smirk returned for a split second before his face morphed to all business. "Give me one good reason to trust your organization again."

"Simple," she said. "Me."

Brewer exhaled sharply. "You do come in handy when a bullet shoots past my right side."

"Give me another shot, and if I fail, I'll figure out a way to go to your safe place," she offered. "Are we good?"

"Good." The one word spoken with finality said there'd be no going back if her second attempt didn't pan out.

To be fair, his life was on the line. Would she handle the situation differently if the shoe were on the other foot? Would she blindly trust someone else with her life? Probably not.

So, she could cut him some slack for digging his heels in and leaning into his stubborn side.

"Give me a few more minutes and I'll have a plan for us," she said. "Deal?"

His nod was almost imperceptible. He was agreeing against his better judgment, according to the questioning look in his eyes. What could she say? The man had beautiful eyes. Eyes she could stare into for days.

And probably a whole lot of women said the same thing. Did the same thing.

Anyway, moving on. She didn't have time for stargazing.

Within seven minutes, she had a new plan. It required a new vehicle, which would also show up in seven minutes. One more seven and she might believe her luck was starting to change.

Her cell buzzed. She checked the screen. Her supervisor was calling, so she answered.

"Marshal Remington here," Crystal said. It was her standard answer, confirming with her superior officer, Elise Fissile, that she was still in charge of her phone. It was their code.

"Everyone all right?" Elise asked.

"Perp is in cuffs, and the witness and I are fine," she

confirmed. "My witness lost a shirt in the process. He'll need more clothing aside from the few things he has in his bag." He couldn't exactly blend in with a ripped shirt. It was bad enough that his hot bod and chiseled jawline drew attention if they had to be in a public place. He didn't exactly make it easy to travel incognito.

"Done," Elise said. "I have a dark blue Chevy Tahoe heading your way. In the dashboard will be a folder with cash and new identities inside."

"Okay," Crystal said. "I'll confirm as soon as I have the vehicle in my possession."

"I'm putting you in a motel off Harry Hines Boulevard for the night," Elise informed.

She groaned. Talk about a fall from grace. They were going from a spacious town house with hardwood flooring and granite countertops to a roach motel. *Great.* Looked like Crystal would be sleeping with one eye open tonight. She hated cockroaches.

"We can do that," she finally said, searching her thoughts for other options. Checking into the motel didn't mean she had to sleep there. Once she was alone with Brewer, she would ask if he had another idea.

"The bounty on your witness's head is half a million dollars, by the way." Elise was probably picking up the roll of Tums sitting on top of her desk. Every time she delivered bad news, she popped one.

"That's a lot of money for a starting bid." The price would go up.

"The FBI is involved, so watch out for one of their agents," her boss continued without missing a beat.

"Do I get a name?" Crystal asked.

"I'm working on it," Elise supplied. "But they aren't in full cooperation mode after Mahone outed one of their agents by accident last month. The director and I are barely on speaking terms right now."

"Which is understandable under the circumstances."

"Mahone tried to get himself reassigned to assist you in case this gets bigger than one marshal," Elise said, then paused. Her supervisor was no doubt waiting for a reaction. There were rules against two marshals in the same division having a personal relationship. Rules that were in place for good reason.

"Do we have enough personnel to put two marshals on this case?" Crystal asked, keeping her voice as level as possible. Unaffected. She had to come across like she didn't care one way or the other.

"No." Elise's suspicions had been raised since Lucas wasn't exactly being discreet about his attachment to her. The last thing Crystal needed in her file was a reprimand for dating a coworker. Not to mention the fact they weren't a couple any longer and hadn't been since before his transfer.

And she had bigger priorities in her personal life right now. Her grandparents needed her, and she felt guilty as hell for being here and not there. She needed to go home to Mesa Point and park it until they were better. The doctor had no idea how long that might take or if it would even happen in all honesty, but Crystal refused to give up hope when hope was all she had.

"So, you're okay on your own with the witness?" Elise continued.

Crystal wasn't sure *okay* was the right word to use, but she'd figure it out. "No problem."

THE FIGHT WITH the bounty hunter marked the first time Brewer had been physically challenged since losing part of his leg. He'd come out all right. A spot the size of a baseball on his left rib cage where he'd taken a knee already hurt like hell. The bruise would make twisting and bending painful. At least his rib wasn't cracked. Or at least not that he could tell.

He'd become good at assessing his injuries over the years. Adrenaline had gotten him far this evening, but the boost was already wearing thin. Exhaustion settled in as a replacement. Brewer was bone tired.

Crystal joined him in the kitchen where he'd propped himself up, back against the wall. His eyes were closed, causing every other sense to come alive to make up for the momentary sight loss. Bodies, when he really thought about it, could be amazing. Too bad they couldn't regrow broken or missing parts.

"What's the plan, boss?" he asked when she stopped a couple feet in front of him.

Slowly he opened his eyes, doing his level best not to notice full, kissable lips. Or the way her tongue slicked across them before she spoke, leaving a silky trail.

Crystal made eyes at him. "I have a new place, but I'm not sleeping there." She shivered.

"That bad?" He barely held back a chuckle at her physical response. Must've been bad if she was having this kind of reaction to it.

"Roach motel," she said, then winced. "I can't."

"Do you have a better idea?" he asked on a laugh. Movement hurt. The bruise forming was going to be a doozy.

"Figured I'd ask you first," she admitted. He appreciated the trust she'd given in that statement.

"I have the place I mentioned before, but it might be too far away," he stated. "It's completely off the grid."

Crystal shifted her weight from her left foot to her right. He'd never noticed feet as much as he did now. It was a strange fact. Once he'd lost his foot, he couldn't stop checking out everyone else's. Brains did interesting things sometimes. He figured he could study his for the rest of his life and still know a fraction of its capabilities.

At least she was considering the option.

"*Off the grid* sounds really tempting right now," she said after a thoughtful pause. "But I should probably stay in range so I can provide updates to my boss. Otherwise, we could end up stranded with no support or backup."

"You've proven to be all the backup I need," he muttered.

"Thanks for the compliment." Her cheeks turned three shades of red, which shouldn't have been as sexy as hell.

"How about taking a drive and seeing where we end up?"

He didn't hate the idea.

"Okay," he said.

"My superior is having a Chevy Tahoe delivered in the next—" she checked her watch "—two minutes."

"We're ditching the old ride?"

"Just in case we were followed," she said. "I didn't see anyone." The look of failure that crossed her features was a little too familiar.

He was about to be a hypocrite but decided to say it anyway. "If we were followed, it wasn't your fault."

"Doesn't matter," she quipped. "It was my responsibility."

For once, Brewer didn't have a comeback. In fact, he understood her logic completely. Hell, it was the same logic he used to beat himself up over what happened overseas. The guilt was real. The sense of failure was real. The losing sleep at night over past mistakes was real.

The only thing he could say in all honesty was "You're

good at your job. No one is perfect. Not even you. This could have happened to anybody. This could have happened to me if I'd been out here alone. And then where would I be?"

"You?" The look of surprise on her face caught him off guard. "No. You would be just fine."

Without expanding, she turned toward the back door. "No reason to stick around here any longer. Our Tahoe is pulling into the alley now."

As much as Brewer appreciated the vote of confidence, *fine* wasn't the word he would use to describe not hearing a bullet whiz past his ear. He'd never needed anyone in his life, so this new reality had him off his game.

Did he need Crystal Remington? Or could he still strike out on his own and keep himself safe?

Chapter Six

Crystal met the driver in the alley, thanked him, and then climbed into the driver's seat. Walking away from Brewer when he was busy complimenting her had been necessary. The fact that he felt the need to bolster her confidence shouldn't have irritated her. But it did.

Being on edge had more to do with her grandparents than this high-profile case. Their conditions weighed heavily on her thoughts. Guilt sat like a wet blanket around her shoulders for working while they were in the hospital. Grandpa Lor wouldn't have had it any other way, though. He would give her a hard time for taking work off—even if she could—so she could sit around a hospital room and watch him breathe. The knowledge made being on the job a little easier.

Brewer appeared at the back door, once again taking up the entire frame. The man was like looking across a lake, placid on the surface with a whole lot brewing underneath. It was the stuff underneath that concerned her.

At least they'd built a tentative bridge of trust today. She couldn't say for certain that meant he would stick around, but she had more confidence that he was giving witness protection a chance. Giving *her* a chance.

Without a whole lot of ceremony, he slipped into the

passenger seat, placed his rucksack at his feet, and then buckled in.

"Hungry?" she asked, thinking a burger and fries sounded almost too good right now. They could swing by a drive-through if she had him hide his face.

"Yes," he conceded. Quiet Brewer was back. Brooding?

"Whataburger sound good?"

"Sure," he said, distracted.

Crystal was an overthinking specialist, so she recognized the trait in others. But right now, she sat at the mouth of the alley unsure of which way to turn. "Left or right?"

"You're asking me?"

"Never mind," she said, turning left as she remembered it was the long way out of the neighborhood. She tapped the steering wheel with her thumb. Going out a different way in a different vehicle was good. There would be more bounty hunters stepping up to the challenge as word spread, especially with a price as high as the one on his head. Keeping him alive to collect worked in her favor.

She mentally shook off the thought.

There was no way Crystal was losing Brewer. "Tell me more about the guy who hooked you up with the job."

"Trent Thomas?"

She nodded.

"We grew up in the same town. Although I wouldn't call us friends. I wasn't exactly Mr. Popular back then."

The file on Brewer said he'd confused himself for a boxer in his youth. "You ever consider going pro?" she quipped.

"Pro?"

"Boxing. I read that you liked to punch first, ask questions later," she said. It wasn't a judgment, just fact.

"Growing up a punching bag for my old man gave me

enough practice." His voice held no emotion. He could have been reading the contents of a cereal box for how little feeling came across.

"You ever reconcile with your father?" she asked.

"Why would I? He wasn't there for me when I was growing up," he said with brutal honesty.

Crystal could relate.

"You got quiet all of a sudden," Brewer pointed out.

She nodded. "Let's just say that I can relate to having a deadbeat for a dad." But didn't a little piece of everyone wish their parent could be there for them? "I never thought about the man until the accident."

"You said he called but did he show up at the hospital?"

"Not to my knowledge. He's too good to darken the door of Mesa Point," she said, then realized she'd just said her hometown out loud. Normally she kept personal information to herself with a witness. "That's where my grandparents live, and it's where I'm from."

"Forgive me for saying but the bastard doesn't deserve to know you or your family if you ask me."

She couldn't argue his point. Even though a growing part of her wanted to let go of the very real pain in her chest at the mention of her father. He might not have deserved her forgiveness, but she wanted peace. Would forgiving the man bring her peace of mind?

Since this was going nowhere, she circled the conversation back around to Trent. "Tell me more about your buddy."

"What's to tell?" He fidgeted with the strap on his rucksack. "Like I said, we weren't buddies back in Galveston— but then I didn't have friends then. I was classified as a loner by my guidance counselor."

"Were you?"

"A loner?" The question was rhetorical. "Hell yes. I went from this skinny kid who got picked on to someone who could snap a neck like that." He snapped his fingers for emphasis. "Kids left me alone after that."

"But you still fought," she said.

"Anyone and everyone who had a bone to pick with me." Brewer talked like that was as normal as day and not a cry for help. Her heart went out to him. With two siblings and three cousins all close in age, she'd been insulated from bullying except for the snide comments about her dad and being an orphan. Kids could be cruel. No one got out of childhood without having their feelings hurt by their peers at one point or another. Outright bullying, relentless bullying was a different story. She tensed thinking about the cruelty and the damage it left behind. She'd seen the effects. Depression. Teen suicide.

"I'm sorry that happened to you," she said and meant it.

"It's fine," he said with forced conviction.

"No, it's not. It's never fine. It's awful, and no one should have to deal with it, least of all teenagers who already have enough pressure."

"I survived," he said. His voice a study in measured calm. Forced calm?

BREWER CHECKED THE side-view mirror as he bit back a yawn.

"Whataburger is a couple of blocks from here," Crystal said. "Then we can figure out a place to grab some sleep."

"Sounds like a plan to me," he said. The other subject was closed. He'd had a bad childhood; one he wouldn't wish on his worst enemy. It happened. He wasn't the only one. Sitting around being angry didn't change it. Which was why he'd moved on.

No other words were spoken as Crystal drove the few blocks and then pulled into the drive-through. Even at this hour, there was a long line.

"How do you know Dallas so well if you're from Mesa... wherever?"

"Point," she supplied. "It's Mesa Point. And I come here all the time for work."

"Hiding witnesses?"

"That and other things," she said.

"I thought that's all marshals did," he said. "Witness protection, right?"

A smile broke across her face. "We do a whole lot more than that, but that's what everyone thinks." She glanced over, and those simple few seconds stirred something deep inside his chest. He dismissed the feeling as being overly tired.

"What else do you do?"

"Protect federal judges," she continued with the kind of pride he'd felt at serving his country once he'd gotten over his anger. "We track down felons and arrest them, bring them to justice. Then there's prisoner transport to add to the list." She pulled up to the order box as she turned to him. "What'll it be? Dinner is on me tonight."

He couldn't help but chuckle before giving his order of a jalapeño burger with the works and fries. What could he say? The marshal was intelligent and funny, not to mention one of the most beautiful women he'd laid eyes on. If he complimented her on her looks, she would probably deny them.

Crystal ordered the avocado-and-bacon burger along with an order of fries.

"You said the blood on your shirt is from the bounty

hunter," she said once out of earshot from the order box. "Have you checked your right shoulder?"

"I did while you were on the call," he admitted.

"And?"

"It's not much more than a scratch," he said, dismissing the fact it could be a real injury. He'd been nicked by the bullet his right ear had failed to warn him about. He glanced over at the blood stain slowly flowering on his shoulder. Okay, maybe more than a scratch. All he needed was a needle and fishing line to sew it up. "You have a first-aid kit somewhere in the supplies you requested, right?"

"Yes," she said, drawing out the word.

"That's all I need to take care of it," he responded. "It's nothing a good Band-Aid can't fix." Softening the injury wasn't an outright lie so much as meant to put Crystal's mind at ease. Right now, all her focus needed to go toward keeping them both alive. If Crane got his way, Brewer would be dead by morning. Or worse, alive and tortured to the point that death would be a relief.

Men like Crane showed no mercy. Something was missing inside that made them ruthless. Heart? Conscience?

Those came to mind first, but it was even deeper than that. A soul?

"Your file says you were on the job for six months," Crystal said, shifting the topic.

"Give or take," he admitted.

"Why didn't you just quit?" she asked. "You could have saved yourself all this stress and drama if you'd walked away. You could have relocated and started a new life. Gone off the grid like you mentioned before."

"Good questions," he said. "Quitting was never an option for me."

"Why not?" she pressed. "A whole lot of people, probably most, wouldn't dare go up against someone like Crane. And for good reason. He's one of the worst. He has long reach. The only person in the area who could hold his own against the man is Michael Mylett's organization."

"True," he agreed. "Everything you said is fact."

"Have you ever had interactions with Mylett?" she asked.

He shook his head. "I know of him, but I didn't have a reason to speak to him."

"How does Trent know Crane?" she pushed.

The vehicle in front of them moved up a car length and she advised him to keep his face hidden as they neared the window.

"Through a second cousin," Brewer said. "I reached out to Trent to see if he knew anyone who was hiring. He got back to me a couple days later after putting out a few feelers with his relatives."

"Trent wasn't aware of his criminal enterprise?" she asked, not buying that he wasn't. Crane must have trusted Trent's cousin or he wouldn't have taken him up on his suggestion to hire Brewer.

"Said he wasn't and I believe him," Brewer said, sounding defensive. "You asked me why I didn't just walk away from Crane. Believe it or not, I didn't have a lot of honor in my actions growing up," he admitted. "There my aunt was, though. Standing beside me. Telling me that I would do better next time." The memories brought tears to the backs of his eyes. Brewer didn't cry. "How would I ever be able to go home again, look her in the eye if I ran away when I could save lives?"

"That's an honorable thing to say," she said. "Even more honorable to stand by your words."

"It's the right thing to do," he said dismissively. He never thought of himself as anything but a normal human doing his best to stay on the right track, make his aunt proud.

"Which doesn't exactly make it easy," Crystal pointed out.

"It's simple when you break it down to what's right or wrong," he countered. "Walking away, letting this man continue to get away with murder, would have kept me awake nights. Being killed would be better than never sleeping again."

"Still, there's a lot of honor in what you're doing," she said.

The respect in Crystal's voice did little to tamp down his growing attraction to the marshal. A part of him was starting to wish there could be something between them no matter how impossible that might be.

Or was it?

Chapter Seven

Crystal was thoroughly impressed by her witness. She protected everyone with the same integrity. However, it wasn't uncommon for her to be charged with keeping a criminal alive to testify against an even bigger criminal. Low-level criminals sometimes turned against their bosses. There was always a story behind the reason that often times ended up being about self-preservation. The low-level criminal had messed up, and then his or her head ended up on the chopping block. Or their family was threatened. WITSEC was self-preservation for those types.

Then there were innocent folks who'd been in the wrong place at the wrong time, causing them to witness a crime in process. Protecting someone who hadn't asked for any of this always hit Crystal square in the chest.

The vehicle in front moved up, so Crystal did the same. She rolled down her window. The food smell filled the cab of the Tahoe and made her stomach growl.

And then there was Brewer. He had experience with war. He'd unwittingly gone to work for a criminal, figured it out, and then turned state's witness to lock the bastard behind bars for the rest of his life.

Brewer had to be fully aware that he could be hunted long after the trial. Crane had long arms, in a manner of speaking, and a man like him would lose all street credibility if he allowed Brewer to get away with testifying and then staying alive.

All Brewer had in the world was his aunt, who was safely tucked away. He could go into the program when the trial was all said and done. He could be given a new identity, a new job, a new lease on life.

Or—and this was the most likely scenario—he could disappear all by himself. He could disappear off the grid. She had no doubt he would survive. There were still remote places in America where a person could go to get lost. Then there was Canada. He could set up camp in the vast wilderness there. Facing wildlife had to be more appealing than always looking over his shoulder for someone in the scumbag organization he'd worked for to find him and kill him.

Would he be able to walk away from his aunt? Leave her without knowing if she would be all right? He wouldn't be able to afford twenty-four-hour security. Not even if he handed over his entire paycheck while he slept on the soil and ate from the land. With her age and general health, he wouldn't be able to take her with him.

"Hey," he said to her, breaking through the noise in her head.

She looked over at him. He nodded toward the front of the Tahoe. Oh. Right. She'd been so lost in thought she didn't realize it was her turn to move up.

After paying for the food and drinks, she pulled up and then found a parking spot.

"Mind if we eat right now?" she asked, not waiting to dig into one of the bags.

"I was thinking the same thing," he said with a smile

that most likely had women forming lines for the chance to spend time with him.

For the next few minutes, nothing mattered but devouring burgers and fries.

Since she hated the smell of food lingering in a vehicle, she grabbed the bags and then headed to the trash can positioned next to the door of the fast-food joint. From the cab, she heard Brewer protest, saying he could do it. She waved him off, needing to stretch her legs a bit. Plus, she was stalling for time.

No magical ideas came to her on the walk back and forth, but it was still nice to get fresh air.

"What had you so quiet in the line earlier?" Brewer asked after she reclaimed her seat.

Crystal might as well come clean. "I was just thinking about how a lot of the witnesses I protect come to me in order to save themselves. I'm the lesser of two evils, if that makes sense."

He nodded that it did.

"And here you are truly placing yourself in harm's way in order to do the right thing," she said.

Risking a glance, she could have sworn his cheeks flooded with embarrassment. It was fleeting, and he regained composure within seconds.

"It's the right thing to do," he said. "It's not hard."

"Oh, but it is," she countered. "And you deserve credit for being an honorable person."

He sat there quiet for a long moment. "I had a lot to make up for from my youth."

With his father treating Brewer like a punching bag instead of a person, she was surprised all the goodness hadn't been beaten out of him. She'd come across plenty of folks in her line of work who used a bad childhood as the reason they'd turned to crime.

Everyone had a choice. Everyone experienced trauma in one way or the other. Everyone had the ability to determine right from wrong.

So, she never let someone off the hook easily.

"Since we're talking about the past," he hedged. "Do you ever wonder what your life would have turned out like if your mom was still alive?"

"No," she said, surprised at how quickly he'd turned the tables on her. "Why would I? It would only be a waste of time."

He nodded, but it was more like concession.

"My dad was another story," she continued. "I made up all kinds of stories in my head about why he had to leave, like he was some kind of saint who was out making the world a better place and had to keep us in a secure location. I used to wake up on my birthdays certain the man would walk through the door with an armload of presents. I gave him all kinds of jobs. Adventurer. There were times when I decided he couldn't contact me because he was in some kind of remote jungle, saving someone's life. He was always the hero who would ride in on the white horse someday to rescue us."

Brewer reached over the console and took her by the hand. Hers was small by comparison. The moment of silence between them after her skin's reaction to his touch felt like the most intimate moment of her life.

How could that be?

Since this man possessed superpowers that scared the hell out of her, she pulled her hand back and thanked him.

This time, when he nodded, she saw hurt in his eyes.

"We should get back on the road," she said. "It's a mistake to sit in one place too long."

"Okay," he said, his voice sounded gruff now. His deep timbre sent warmth all through her body. Even now. Even when his voice was clipped and there was a trace of hurt in his tone.

Had another wall come up between them?

BREWER HAD NO idea why Crystal had withdrawn her hand but after making physical contact decided the move was probably for the best. Electrical aftershocks still rocked his hand and arm even after a minute passed.

"Do you consider yourself an outside person?" Crystal asked.

"I can camp with the best of 'em. Why?" Was she about to ditch the Tahoe and head for the woods? They were in Dallas, so there were no mountains. Everything here was flat, which worked to their advantage. No twisty roads to make them worry about something or someone lurking around the next bend. No fog to blind them until they were right up on someone. And not many trees to hide behind.

There were, however, wide-open skies. Even at night, he felt the openness. And there were vehicles everywhere, day and night. It didn't matter. Someone was on the roads, making it easier to blend in.

The Tahoe had blacked-out windows despite the otherwise soccer-mom look. Glancing at the fast-food line, there'd been exactly three Tahoes with soccer emblems on the back window along with the names of the players scrolled underneath.

If Brewer ever had kids, their names would not be stamped on the back of the family vehicle. It seemed like the easiest way to get his kid stolen. The kidnapper already had the kid's name and some information about him or her. The more information a perp had, the easier it would be to convince the kid that they already knew each other. Or that the perp knew the kid's parents.

Brewer caught himself right there and stopped the train of thought. Him with a kid? He'd never once considered it. Karma was hell, and he'd racked up too much bad karma during his youth. His own kid would most likely have personality traits that would be payback.

Plus, he'd never once envisioned himself as a father. His bad genes needed to die with him. And now that he wasn't a whole man any longer, he couldn't imagine anyone would want to spend their life with him.

"I was thinking we could find a spot, park, and lean the seats back," she said. "The problem is going to be finding a place out of the way enough not to draw attention."

"Or we could do it the other way," he stated. "We could find a small neighborhood that has cars lined up on the streets and slip in between a couple of big trucks."

"That would be Garland or Richardson," she said with a spark in her voice that shouldn't have caused the knot in his chest to tighten as much as it did.

Adding to Crystal's positive traits was her voice. She had the kind of laugh that was like waking up to a spring morning after a rain shower, the air clean and crisp.

Before he tripped down that rabbit hole, he cleared his throat and grounded himself in the reality that she was there as his protection from a ruthless criminal.

Brewer glanced at the rearview mirror and could have sworn he recognized someone a couple of cars back. "We might have picked up a tail."

Crystal muttered a curse. "I made a mistake keeping us in the area too long." She smacked the wheel with her right palm. "I shouldn't have done that."

Was she always so hard on herself?

"We're a team," he corrected. "Your mistakes are my mistakes. Got it?"

"We can talk about that later," she said, cutting a hard right at the next light as it turned red. "Let's see if this sonofabitch follows."

The vehicle made the turn, squealing the tires as it rounded the corner.

"At least we know what we're dealing with now," she said. "I need to call this in and get some help."

"Or we could handle this on our own."

"You're not used to following protocol," she said. "I get that. But my job is on the line, and it's all I have right now. I won't risk it."

Crystal cut a hard left, entering a quiet neighborhood. A cul-de-sac?

Brewer grunted. "Ever hear of soldiers following orders?"

"Of course," she admitted.

"They're not called suggestions for a reason," he quipped, more offended than he probably should've been. Hell, everything put his guard up since the blast. A little voice in the back of his mind asked if he was starting to get tired of always being tense. The answer would be yes.

Being chased brought back a flood of memories. Brewer reached for the grab handle and then wrapped his fingers around it until his knuckles turned white.

"Everything all right over there?" Crystal asked after glancing over at him.

Pride kept him from admitting just how not okay he was right now. "Fine."

"What's happening, Brewer?"

"Nothing."

"We can't work well together as a team if you lie to me or keep me in the dark," she countered.

Damn. She was right. He knew it. But opening up right now would lead to a whole can of worms being dumped out when she needed to focus.

"I can handle it," he reassured. "But yeah, a lot's going through my head right now." It was the best way to describe what was happening. Flashes, memories, panic. Those three words instantly came to mind as a fresh wave of guilt assaulted him. *Stay in the present, Brewer.*

This was his cross to bear since he was the one to survive when the others hadn't. He reached down for the strap of his rucksack. Rubbed it in between his thumb and forefinger on his left hand. And then had to repeat the move with his right hand. Next, he touched the dashboard with one hand and then the other before reaching for the grab handle again.

The urge to continue what he'd just done in a repetitive cycle was almost overwhelming.

"Whatever is going on is okay with me," Crystal said in a calm, reassuring voice. "You don't have to talk about it. I just want you to know that I'm here if you change your mind or if talking helps."

Man, was he embarrassed to admit the level of psychosis battling it out inside him. More than anything, he wanted to repeat the touch cycle. The fact that he'd stopped himself from touching everything in sequence revved up his stress.

He glanced at the side-view mirror as a pair of headlights came charging toward them. "You have bigger problems to worry about right now instead of what's going on inside my head."

Crystal checked her rearview and muttered the exact same curse he was thinking. "Hold on, okay?"

It was dark on the street she'd turned down save for one streetlight at the curve of the cul-de-sac.

How the hell was she going to get them out of this mess with his brain being absolutely no help?

Take a deep breath, Brewer.

Chapter Eight

Crystal saw no other out as she reached the cul-de-sac. The yards here looked to be decent size—quarter of an acre to half acre. Fences weren't the normal eight-foot privacy fences like much of Dallas and surrounding cities had.

This might've been a trap, but she was short on options. So, she cut the wheel right onto the paved driveway that led to the back of a random person's house. Destroying civilian property could get her in more trouble than she wanted to consider, so she didn't. She blocked that out of her mind and went into sheer survival mode.

Keeping her witness alive trumped everything else.

Making a hard right, she drove beside the house with no lights on. The sleepy neighborhood looked to be one of those that rolled-up the streets after eight thirty every evening, a place where parents still allowed their children to play out front in the yard.

Roaring through their backyards at half past midnight would scare the neighbors, not to mention wake them. The law would be called. She was putting a spotlight on her activities, which could end up putting her in the hot seat with her boss.

Losing a witness was far worse than any punishment Elise could devise.

As she cut around the back of the house, she gunned the engine. Navigating around trees and bright yellow-and-blue toy cars before almost landing in the pool, she gripped the steering wheel tighter.

It dawned on her based on how quiet Brewer became that a battle was going on inside his thoughts. This must've taken him back to the incident that had ended his military career. She almost blurted out another curse as she swerved around the house and risked a glance back.

The chorus of dogs barking set against the backdrop of lights flipping on inside the homes tightened the knot in her chest. The knot warned that not everything was going to turn out all right.

It had been lodged there since hearing about her grand-parents' vehicle accident and was determined to take root inside her chest.

Risking a glance behind as she made the turn, she saw the moment the car that had been following her nailed a tree. She pumped a fist in the air before quickly returning both hands to the steering wheel.

An adrenaline boost collided with dopamine release, giving her a euphoria that only sex with Brewer could beat. Cancel that thought—she wasn't now or ever having sex with her witness. Not only would that be unprofessional but having the best sex of her life with someone who would disappear wasn't her best idea.

Crystal shoved those unproductive thoughts aside and focused on the stretch of road ahead as she navigated back onto the street.

Before the car could untangle itself from the tree and catch up to her, she flew out of the neighborhood. This future write-up caused a wave of dread to wash over her.

The behind-chewing that was coming would be worth it, though.

They were safe from threat.

"Good driving back there," Brewer said as she navigated back to a main road. Laced with respect, she appreciated those words coming from someone like him. The man was no stranger to battle and had, no doubt, been in worse situations.

"Thank you," she said. "We're not out of the woods yet."

"No, but sticking together was a good decision on my part," he admitted.

She didn't want those words to reach into her and warm the cold places in her chest—places that had caused her to leave every past relationship.

"That means a lot, Brewer."

"Bounty hunters are going to come out of the woodwork," he surmised.

"True."

He was right. No doubt about it. The amount of money on the line would draw out a whole lot of scumbags looking to make a buck and not afraid to break a few laws or heads in the process.

"Don't tell me that you're giving up," she said.

"Never," came the fast response. He studied the side-view mirror. "It just means we have to be more careful. And, as much as I hate to say it, lose the Tahoe and any other vehicle related to the Marshals Service."

"Why is that?" Every marshal on the job had a plan, one they incorporated when everything had gone to hell in a hand basket and they needed to disappear. Inside the trunk of her service vehicle, Crystal kept her real passport, a fake-identity passport that would get her through any major international airport without being stopped, a wad of cash, burner phone, and keys. The keys were for a safe vehicle to drive to and from the airport. Since going through proper channels wasn't paying off, should she circle back and use hers so her witness could make it to his court date?

Something niggled at the back of her mind. She couldn't quite put her finger on it.

"How did the guy back in the car know we'd changed vehicles?" he asked.

"Are you suggesting someone on the inside could be handing out information about us because—"

"I'm not disagreeing that could be the case," he interrupted. "Or someone has figured out how to get through the encryption in your cell phone to follow us."

"That's it," she said out loud.

"What?"

"Give me your cell phone," she stated, holding out a hand.

"Why?"

"Because you might be the one being tracked," she said. "Have you made any calls with it since we've been together?"

"No," he denied. "Not to anyone who would compromise our position."

"Does that mean yes?"

"Yes," he retracted. "I called my buddy Trent back at the diner so he could set me up with a place off the grid."

"The one who got you the job in the first place?" she asked, shocked.

"Yes," he said. "But I don't see how that—"

Brewer cursed.

"They might have tapped his cell phone," he said out loud after muttering a few choice words.

"They would absolutely tap into his line to see if you

reached out to him," she said. "But if he has a connection to them, they would probably tap his line anyway."

"There's one way to test the theory."

Crystal glanced over at Brewer to see if he was serious. The answer came quickly—yes, he was.

"What are you proposing?" she asked as the knot tightened.

TRENT'S LINE WOULD be encrypted. Hacking into his phone would require skill. Then again, a multimillion-dollar operation would have the funds to hire the best. And Trent had been a foot soldier, not predictable in the military. His skill set would be no match for an experienced tech person's, and he couldn't match what the organization could afford to pay for an individual, which was the reason the person with the most money usually won.

But this wasn't the time to debate economics.

"We need to find a spot where we can leave the burner phone and then watch to see who shows up," he said.

"I knew you would say something like that," she stated. "Isn't it just easier to ditch your phone?"

"Not if I need to get into contact with Trent again," he pointed out. His friend felt bad enough for getting Brewer into this mess. Not knowing whether Brewer was alive or dead would cause more unnecessary stress. Plus, he intended to have Trent check on his aunt at some point to make sure she was fine and didn't need anything. Trent was all he had.

"Doesn't seem like a good idea, Brewer."

"Why not?" he asked.

Crystal didn't respond to his question. Instead, she kept

her gaze on the stretch of road in front of them. "You need sleep."

"So do you," he said. "Neither of us will get it until we find out if my phone is causing a problem for us."

"How about this," she said after a thoughtful pause. "We put the phone somewhere safe, and then we find another location to get sleep. How does that sound?"

"We could figure out a way to find out if anyone showed up," he said.

"It's too late for a bank vault, but we could set up a camera to see who shows," she said. "I haven't had a chance to circle back to find out the first bounty hunter's name yet. Or get the debrief."

"You expect a man like him to talk?" he asked.

"I guess not," she said. "Depends on his situation, though. If he has a kid who needs medical attention, you'd be surprised at what we can get from a person."

"What are the odds?"

She sighed sharply. "I guess not so good, but I always circle back. Once in a blue moon, you hit a jackpot."

"While you play the slots over there, I'll use my phone as bait," he said. "We'll see who gets something on the other end of the line first."

"Is that a challenge?" she asked as a smile fought to replace the frown that he was beginning to believe might be permanent.

"You always this sarcastic?" she quipped.

"Why? Does it bother you?"

"No," she said. "I prefer to talk to someone with a sense of humor." She paused a beat. "Looks like I'll be waiting a long time now that I'm stuck with you."

Brewer laughed, and it broke up some of the tension

block—tension that felt like hardened concrete—in his chest that had made it so hard to breathe a few minutes ago. "How about we compromise?"

"What do you propose?" she asked.

"Like you said, hide the phone, set up cameras, and let's get some sleep." He might not've needed it, but she certainly did. The news about her grandparents affected her despite her arguments to the contrary. It didn't make her bad at her job, but the worry lines etched into her forehead weren't about him and his situation. The only person who would put those there for him was his aunt, so he couldn't imagine if she was in a coma and her future uncertain. He owed it to Crystal for all the sacrifices she was making for him.

It was odd when he really thought about it. His military career had been about doing the same for others. Volunteering to put his life on the line to preserve a way of life for others came down to putting a face to the why. His aunt was the reason he'd gone into the military in order to get his act together. Her face came to him before he entered into a situation that put his life on the line.

She had no one to look out for her if he didn't come home. And now he was the reason she was in danger. Talk about a hard pill to swallow.

"Do you have a location in mind?" she asked.

"Why not make this easy on ourselves? Why not secure my phone where there will already be cameras? I'm sure you could finagle getting a hotel manager to show us video if you flashed your badge."

"I can get more than that for flashing my smile," she said, causing a wave of jealousy to stab him in the heart. What was that about?

"No doubt," he said, trying to tamp down his reaction to

the suggestion. There was no sexual innuendo about it, but he was certain her smile could open a lot of doors. Doors he didn't like sitting back and watching as they opened.

He had no designs on Crystal Remington. *Marshal Remington*, the tiny voice in the back of his mind corrected.

This seemed like a good time to remind himself she wasn't here as a volunteer or a date. Protecting him was her job—a job that she seemed to be very good at and took very seriously. Because of that job, the two of them would part ways once he was safely delivered to trial on a date yet to be determined. Reading anything else into the situation wouldn't just be foolish, it would be dangerous. Getting his hopes up was a risk he didn't intend to take. One more disappointment and he'd be wrecked. He'd already lost too much in the men who'd been like brothers. In his own body with his leg and his hearing.

Brewer sensed that losing Crystal, if he opened his heart to her, would be the last straw. The one thing to break him.

No way. No matter how strong the pull toward Crystal might be. No matter how difficult fighting the attraction might be. No matter how much he wanted to lean into it and claim those pink lips of hers as his.

He wouldn't.

Couldn't.

Refused.

Chapter Nine

Crystal needed to get them out of the Tahoe. They'd been circling around downtown Dallas for twenty minutes now. One-way street after one-way street. The DART Rail came to mind. The Pearl/Arts District Station was the closest to their current location. If memory served, that one was located on Bryan Street.

Stopped at a red light, she grabbed her cell phone and pulled up the map feature. From the corner of her eye, she noticed Brewer staring at her with a curious look on his face. "I have an idea."

She pulled over after making the next right turn.

"We need to ditch this vehicle," she pointed out.

"Agreed," he said. "What's the idea?"

"How do you feel about riding a train?"

"Cool with me," he said. His tone told her he was smiling.

She parked the Tahoe. "Grab all your stuff. We're not coming back to this vehicle again." The fact that someone was on their tail so quickly after the town house unnerved her. Standard measures weren't enough to stay ahead of this organization. Everything about her plan needed to rise to the next level in order to survive.

Crystal led them to the train station, then hopped onto

the next train. The ticket machine had been too exposed for her to risk standing there to buy tickets. Her badge would be enough to get them by if anyone checked.

The train was empty save for a couple of guys who looked like they'd spent the evening out drinking. Better to have them on the train keeping to themselves than driving.

Both got off on the next stop. For the rest of the ride to the end of the line, it was only Crystal and Brewer in the car they'd chosen. A lucky break.

Those had been too few and far in between for her liking, but she was developing a new plan now.

"Once we check to see if anyone is tracking that phone, we need to find a place to sleep," she surmised.

"Agreed," was all he said, using the word for a second time. He was down to one- or two-word responses at this point. Was he tired? Or losing confidence in her ability to keep him safe? Tired she could live with because exhaustion wore on her too. Loss of confidence might mean he was evaluating his options again. That frustrated her to no end.

Time would tell. In the meantime, she intended to keep a close eye on him.

They exited at the Parker Road Station and then located a parked vehicle in the well-lit parking lot. A Ford truck would do.

"Hand me your cell," Crystal said, standing at the tailgate of the silver Ford F-350.

Brewer fished it from his pocket. "Let me wipe out the contacts, just in case." He tapped the phone screen a few times before handing it over.

Crystal tucked it into the bed of the truck close to the taillight as Brewer studied the area. They needed a good place to hide and a possible quick getaway. The chain-link fence surrounding the parking lot was a good place to get on the opposite side of.

"If someone is watching my phone, we'll know soon," Brewer said, finally using more than a phrase to speak to her. Had he been in deep concentration before, calculating the best plan of attack? Was that the reason he'd become quiet, and not because he wanted to ditch? His aunt must've been on his mind as well. Crystal knew firsthand how difficult it was to be separated from loved ones. Speaking of which, she needed to check in with Duke. The fact that there hadn't been any updates on the group chat worried her.

Brewer's gaze locked onto a point at the northeast corner of the parking lot.

"Let's give it an hour tops before we take off," she said, not liking the exposure. If this convinced Brewer to lose his phone and confirmed her suspicion, it would be worth the risk. She needed to get a little breathing room in between them and the bastards who always seemed a step behind. At this rate, they would catch up. No one could keep outsmarting an enemy with the kind of reach this one had forever. "Okay?"

"Deal," he said. His word was as good as gold, so she wouldn't question the lack of commitment in his tone.

As they walked away from the truck and phone, a couple of figures jumped the fence and headed across the parking lot. Males. Lanky. Teenagers?

The lot was lit up like it was daylight. The last thing Crystal wanted was to have witnesses see her and Brewer, so without debating her next actions she turned to face him. "Go with it, okay?"

Before he could open his mouth to respond, she pushed

up onto her tiptoes and pressed her lips to his. Looping her arms around his neck was probably a mistake since it caused her breasts to press firmly against his solid wall of a chest. The electrical impulses zipping through her body promised the best sex of her life if things moved forward between them.

They wouldn't. But the sudden ache in her body didn't care one way or the other. The spark of need that threatened to engulf her in flames wasn't doused in the least.

Crystal liked the feel of Brewer's lips moving against hers as the young people gave them a wide berth. The move prevented the teens from seeing her and Brewer's faces, and it awakened parts of her that she hadn't realized existed.

Even with the scars, he was gorgeous. Getting to know him had only served to make him even more attractive if that was possible. For once, Crystal knew exactly what she wanted and wanted to go for it, career be damned.

She wouldn't.

Gathering all her willpower, she pulled back enough to break apart. Her heavy breathing matched his.

"Get a room," one of the teens shouted before they both laughed and then took off running.

She couldn't help but laugh. If only it was that simple.

"They're gone," she said to Brewer, who leaned forward and rested his forehead against hers as they both caught their breath.

"I know," he said, his voice a low rumble that sent more of those sensual shock waves rocketing through her.

What could she say? The man's touch, his voice were the equivalent of Fourth of July fireworks to her body. Her soul?

She stopped herself before she could go all-in with the thought.

"We need to get out of here," she whispered, despite the fact her feet refused to move from this spot.

"I know," he repeated.

Neither one budged.

Crystal had to pull on all the strength she could muster to move. To calm the rising panic in her chest, she dropped her hand to reach for his and then linked their fingers. She could say the move was to sell the fact they were a couple to anyone who might be watching. The truth, however, was that no one was around.

Didn't mean they wouldn't be.

BREWER DIDN'T WANT to think too much about the kiss that had just happened—that had *needed* to happen. He'd immediately understood why Crystal had made the move. Blocking their faces from any passersby was a smart move. No witnesses.

A US marshal would be keen on not leaving witnesses who could be pressed for information or, in some extreme cases, tortured. At this point, the young men could honestly say the only folks they saw in the parking lot had been lovers who'd needed to get a room.

The ache in Brewer's body would subside. He tried to convince himself the tsunami of need had a simple explanation. It was because he'd stopped having sex altogether since losing part of his leg, part of himself. He'd come back from overseas less than whole and didn't want to freak someone out by thinking he was something he was not. Seeing his metal shin and foot for the first time had shocked the hell out of him, and it was his body.

Anyone else would likely flip out too. He couldn't talk about it either. How would that come across? *Hey, we've*

been getting along. Think we should move to the next level?
And, uh, by the way, want to see my fake leg?

He wouldn't be able to stomach the look of rejection in
someone else's eyes he'd seen in his own.

No, thanks.

Shaking off the reverie, he kept a firm grip on Crystal's
hand so she could hop the chain-link fence. She used it as
leverage and easily cleared the obstacle. She muttered a
curse after landing on the prickly hedges on the opposite
side of the fence.

With a one-arm hop, Brewer followed suit. The hedges
scraped his good leg, reminding him that he was still alive.
That was pain's job, he reasoned. It told folks when to stop.
Without it, where would he be?

Pain was the reason he pulled his hand from a hot stove
before it burned to the point that it was useless. Pain was the
reason he knew when he'd had enough during a wrestling
match with one of his brothers in arms. And pain was the
reason he was still alive when others were dead.

Trying to shake off the heavy thoughts, he crouched
down low as Crystal tugged at his jacket. She had on a
navy blazer and jeans. The light blue button-down shouldn't
stand out. She had on dark shoes too.

Was it enough to keep her warm on this chilly night?

"You okay?" he asked, checking her for a reaction. Her
body had been warm against his, but that could've been
for another reason. When they'd been standing with their
bodies flush, warmth had flooded him too.

No doubt in his mind it would be amazing to bury himself inside her and forget the world for a few hours. Days?

As much as he wanted...*craved*...her touch, he couldn't
allow it. People who got too close to him died. The fact

had him stressed about his aunt. So far, so good there. But Brewer was always waiting for the other shoe to drop. How long before it would? How long before more bad news struck?

"I'm good," Crystal responded.

He glanced over and realized she was studying him.

"Everything okay, Brewer?"

"Yeah," he said.

"I'm sorry about the kiss," she continued. It must've been the reason she thought he was upset.

"I'm not," he whispered loud enough for her to get the message. "That's the best thing that's happened to me in too long."

The admission embarrassed him. But there it was.

"Me too," came the response. He probably didn't need to hear that because it spurred him on.

Reaching over and taking her hand in his, he brought her palm up to his mouth and planted a kiss there. "I know nothing could ever happen between us."

"Parallel universe maybe," she offered.

"Doesn't mean I don't want it to," he admitted. This time, he wasn't embarrassed.

She squeezed his hand.

"Same here," she whispered. "We both know an attraction might cause a dangerous distraction."

"And yet the body wants what it wants," he countered, and he could almost feel her smiling. Blushing?

"I have no doubt the sex would be amazing," she said in the voice that had a way of breaching the walls erected around his heart.

"That it would," he said quietly. "Except for the fact…"

He started to open up, talk about the fact he wasn't

whole, then decided against it. What good would it do? How did he even start?

"For what?"

A vehicle pulled into the parking lot, moving slowly. It cut its lights off and then circled the interior once as they buried themselves deeper into the hedge. A branch was cutting into the scratch on Brewer's shoulder, a scratch that he'd only recently stemmed the bleeding from.

The vehicle was a white Camry.

The Camry pulled up behind the truck, keeping the lights off. A red flag if ever there was one. Brewer reached for his weapon inside the pocket of his rucksack. Crystal's hand went to the Glock inside her shoulder holster.

Just in case.

He palmed the handle of the SIG Sauer inside his rucksack, noticing how his hand started shaking. That wasn't like him. Stress only made it worse. He'd been a good shooter before. Was everything being slowly taken away from him?

Brewer bit back a curse and tried to will his hand to stop shaking. He'd refused to see the military psychiatrist because they would have told him what he already knew... he had to learn to deal with this new reality, this new person he'd become.

Someone who couldn't depend on his reflexes. Someone who wasn't whole. Someone who didn't deserve to be alive when two in his unit were dead.

Frustration welled up, filling his chest. At that point, something magical happened. His hand stopped shaking.

Thank the stars for small miracles. This new superpower wouldn't bring the rest of his leg back, but it would keep his hand from moving while he fired off a shot. It might keep him alive.

Crystal shifted position, ending up on his right side.

A female exited the driver's side of the Camry, wearing all black. She crouched down low as she moved around the truck. Did she believe they were inside, asleep?

The way she moved stealth-like and with precision said she did this for a living. A female bounty hunter? From this distance, Brewer couldn't get a good look at her facial features. But no one showed up in all black and moved like her unless they meant business.

Was she assessing threat? Trying to confirm her suspicion that they were asleep? Was she about to try the door and shoot?

She had to think there were two of them inside even though she didn't peek into the windows. Not yet anyway.

They should probably disappear before they drew attention, but Brewer was too interested in seeing what this mystery woman planned to do next.

Chapter Ten

The bounty hunter—and that was the only reasonable explanation for the woman's skill set—circled the truck twice before reaching her hand underneath the truck's bed. GPS would pinpoint the phone's location without being exact. She wouldn't know the difference between the bed or the cab based on a tracking app.

What was she up to? Feeling around for the phone?

A second later, she withdrew her hand and then climbed into her vehicle before backing away from the truck. Then, she sat. Waited.

For what?

Crystal's mind conjured up several possibilities. Before she could go down that road too far, a small explosion sounded.

The truck. The woman. An explosive device.

It took all Crystal's self-control not to stand up and go after the woman. There was no movement in the vehicle she drove.

The bounty hunter was trying to flesh them out of the truck. The explosion wasn't big enough to set the truck on fire or cause much of a scene. It was, however, loud and jarring enough to wake anyone who might've been asleep in the truck.

"We shouldn't stick around here," Crystal whispered. How long would it be before the female checked the immediate area in search of them?

Their question has been answered as far as Crystal was concerned—Trent's phone was being monitored.

Again, she questioned how much Brewer could trust his friend. How close were they?

Brewer nodded as he stared at the truck, his gaze intense. Was he wondering the same thing?

"He's in trouble," he whispered before turning to follow her.

They could discuss Trent later. The chill in the air turned to a biting wind. They needed shelter. Looking at her phone wasn't an option. She couldn't afford for the light from the screen to alert the female bounty hunter.

Still in the parking lot, she inched her Camry toward the truck. She must have been expecting them to come out by now. What would she do next?

The entrance to the parking lot was on the opposite side of Crystal and Brewer's current location, which would buy time because they needed to get the hell away from there. Their dark clothing would help them blend into the night as they continued east.

Crystal shivered in the cold as they made their escape, wishing she'd worn more than her standard navy jacket.

Brewer looped an arm around her waist, and she leaned into his warmth as they moved farther away from the parking lot.

"Thank you," she said, praying they wouldn't draw attention as they crossed Avenue K.

"It's two-fold," he commented. "One, you'll stay warmer. And two, the bounty hunter isn't looking for a couple. She's looking for a marshal and me."

Her chest deflated a little at the practical reasoning. He was right on both counts. She was instantly warmer being nestled in the crook of his arm, and this position would be considered unprofessional under different circumstances, so it would throw off Ninja Woman back there if she happened to drive this way.

Crystal prayed the woman headed in any other direction, but especially west, since it was the opposite way they were headed. "Shelter would be nice. Any ideas there?" She knew he would have a few. They could check into a motel along US 75, which would require them circling back the opposite direction. Crossing the station again wasn't an appealing idea. They needed a place close by.

"Can I see the map feature on your phone?" Brewer asked now that his was gone. For his sake, she hoped Trent came out clean despite her suspicions. She decided to hold her tongue until they received more information about Brewer's friend. According to the file, Trent appeared to run an honest landscaping business. She made a note to get a copy of his client list to see if Crane's name was on it. Without a warrant, she would have to ask for it.

Crystal located her cell and then handed it over. Skin-to-skin contact sent more of that electrical current racing through her hand and up her arm.

He studied the phone for a minute, no longer, and then handed it back. "This way."

Walking side by side, she tensed as several vehicles passed by. Brewer reacted by pulling her closer to him in a protective manner. Crystal couldn't remember the last time someone had done that. Needing someone to protect her versus allowing someone to take the lead were two different things. It was nice to feel like someone could handle whatever came their way. Mahone, her ex, was a marshal; he should have made her feel safe in the way Brewer was. They'd spent time together, been in a relationship. And yet she'd always been on alert with Mahone.

What was it about Brewer that had a calming effect on her?

He led them across a busy intersection toward a residential neighborhood and then onto a quiet street. Cars lined both sides. She was just about to ask what the plan was when he turned to the third house they passed. She saw the wisdom. A covered motorboat. They could slip underneath the tarp, which would get them out of the wind, and grab a few hours of sleep before the sun came up.

And then they would have to talk about Trent.

Crystal slipped onto the motorboat. It had a curved bench seat in the back near the motor. The vinyl covering was cold and caused her to shiver as Brewer positioned himself on the floorboard. He grabbed a life vest to use for a pillow and pulled a sweatshirt out of his rucksack. He spread it out beside him.

"You can slide in here next to me if you want," he said, turning onto his side. "Body heat will help keep us from getting too cold. Might even be able to grab some shut-eye."

"Being warm is too good to pass up right now," she admitted as she was hit full force with the memory of how incredible his lips had felt against hers. Crystal cleared her throat to ease the sudden dryness. She'd never acted in an unprofessional manner when it came to her career and had no plans to begin right now. Not even for someone as tempting as Wade Brewer.

The attraction was strange when she really thought about it. Tattooed and looking more like a rebel than anyone she'd

Bounty Hunted

ever get close enough to call a friend, Brewer was not her typical type. Not on the surface. Okay, the man was hotness on a stick, so he was pretty much everyone's type. Who wouldn't fall for a bad boy who looked straight off an underwear-model billboard? Or at the very least drool over the man?

Crystal normally dated clean-cut men who opened doors and probably called their mothers every weekend. Family was important to her and had to be a priority for anyone she dated as well. She might not have spent as much time with hers as she wanted to or probably should've, but that was going to change once this case was over and she delivered Brewer safely to trial.

Facing losing her grandparents had made her realize how precious time was and how fragile life could be. She'd thought they had all the time in the world, that there would be a slow decline and ample time to spend together before it was too late.

A tear spilled from her eye as she positioned herself in the crook of Brewer's arm again. This time, their bodies were flush with each other, providing much-needed warmth. With the canopy pulled taut, they were safe from the winds. No one knew their location.

For the time being, at least, they were safe. With that thought, Crystal closed her eyes and gave in to the exhaustion tugging at the back of her mind.

BREWER IGNORED JUST how right the marshal felt in his arms. Once again, he chalked up their chemistry to going too long without companionship. The kiss they'd shared had barely scratched the surface and yet had turned the moment in the parking lot into something much more.

So much for playing it cool with Crystal Remington. *Marshal Remington*, he felt the need to keep reminding himself.

Her steady, even breathing told him she'd fallen asleep within minutes of settling in next to him. The fact that she was comfortable, out of the elements, and asleep shouldn't have made his chest puff up with pride as much as it did. There was something deep inside, primal, that brought a smile to his face for being able to protect Crystal. Sleeping in someone's presence was the ultimate act of trust.

Maybe he wasn't completely broken, useless to others.

Once this ordeal was over, he needed a new job. The fact that he'd been paid by a corporation had him believing that, early on, Cane's organization had been legit. To be honest, Brewer's head hadn't been on straight when he'd first boarded out of the military. Six months had made a difference. He'd joined a gym and started working out almost immediately. He'd been so focused on what he'd lost and trying to find a way to live as less than his former self that warning signs had slipped past him.

The meetings with all manner of folks should have tipped him off that Victor Crane wasn't on the up and up. What CEO met with guys wearing warmups?

Brewer had driven Crane to cafés. Those made more sense. There'd been breakfast meetings, lunch meetings, and dinner meetings. None of those were red flags in and of themselves.

In the first few weeks, Brewer had been too inside his own head to notice the man he drove around was meeting with thugs as well as others wearing suits. The job had been *ask no questions, get no answers* kind of work. His military training had taught him not to question. The need-to-know policy had trained him to mind his own business and focus on his task or mission.

He wasn't naive. Looking back, he'd been in too much of a brain fog to question Crane. As he'd started to become more aware of his surroundings again, the red flags had popped up. He'd been too invested at that point to walk away without a plan, a plan to ensure his aunt would be safe long after he was gone.

Right now, though, he was more worried about Trent than anything else. Would there be a backlash against him since he'd been the one to recommend Brewer to the job in the first place? Was Crane keeping Trent alive in order to use him to find Brewer?

He needed to have a conversation with his pal about re-locating once this was over. Or, at the very least, lying low. Trent now knew that Crane was the head of an organized crime business.

Brewer needed to figure out a way to keep Trent safe. So far, he'd been concerned with his aunt.

His thoughts bounced to Crystal and her grandparents. She wasn't with them because she was with him. The fact was a bitter pill to swallow.

Could they swing by Mesa Point? Visit the hospital without being detected?

Brewer's injury marked him. Made him easier to pick out of a crowd if he wore shorts instead of jeans.

The Lithuanian must have seen Brewer or had his physical description. He might've been too high up in the organization now that Crane was behind bars to risk going after Brewer himself.

Crystal shifted in her sleep, causing her body to press harder against his. She mumbled something he couldn't quite pick up.

Was it about an ex? Someone she was interested in?

Why did either of those scenarios cause his chest to deflate as fast as it had puffed up? Crystal was a beautiful woman who was intelligent and sharp-minded. There had to be someone in the background despite her saying she wasn't interested in anyone.

Was he being sexist in his thinking that just because she was beautiful there had to be guys around? Maybe.

Still, he couldn't imagine there wouldn't be half a dozen guys circling the stunning marshal, waiting for a green light from her in order to make a move. A woman like her didn't come around but once in a lifetime. On that point, he was certain.

Any single man who knew her but wasn't interested had to be a fool. If Brewer had had a remote chance under different circumstances, he wouldn't have hesitated. She deserved someone in her life who was decisive about being together, who wanted to be with her more than he wanted to breathe air.

Brewer was amused at the rabbit hole he'd just gone down with the marshal.

"Hey," she whispered in a sleepy voice that brought more of him to life than he cared to admit.

"Morning," he said. Hours had passed while he'd been in deep thought, dozing on and off.

The squeak of a screen door opening caused them both to tense.

"I said I'd take out the trash, and that's what I'm doing," a male voice barked.

Were they about to be caught?

Chapter Eleven

Crystal bit back a curse. She held her breath as she listened. The sound of plastic tires on the brown city-issued trash cans against concrete rolled too close to the boat for comfort. Had they closed the tarp properly?

Folks were known to keep shotguns and other weapons on hand despite living in a suburban area. The whole *shoot first, ask questions later* mantra hit a little too close to home. Would she be able to identify herself in time? More importantly, would the man believe her?

It was dark enough to realize clouds had rolled in overnight. The temps had dropped.

Trash Man started whistling. At least it was easier to follow his movements after he situated the trash bin at the end of his front-entry driveway. He made his way back up the short drive, stopping next to the boat.

"I'll be damned," he muttered, the whistling stopped. "What in tarnation is this?"

Crystal felt around for her Glock, palmed the handle. Brewer moved too, stealth-like, no doubt locating his weapon same as her. Glock out, finger hovering over the trigger mechanism, Crystal was ready if it went down.

Of course, she would identify herself first as a US marshal. It went without saying.

Her cell vibrated. Frustration at the timing seethed. It was followed by fear this might be bad news about her grandparents.

On the other hand, the message could be good news about a trial date. The sooner, the better—except for the fact her case would close and she would walk away from Brewer forever. Crystal pushed the thought out of her mind and craned her neck to hear.

She prepared herself for the tarp to go flying off or a shotgun barrel to be stuck inside.

Trash Man picked up whistling again. Whatever had caught his attention must have passed. She slowly exhaled, not budging.

A dog barked rapid-fire. The pet came barreling up to the boat and jumped as it barked.

"What's wrong with Butch?" a female voice shouted.

Crystal imagined Butch was some kind of bully dog, like a pit bull. Something that latched on when it bit and its jaw couldn't be pried open with machinery once it locked.

"Probably another squirrel," Trash Man said, dismissing the dog's attempt to warn them that people were inside their boat.

"Get in here, Butch," the female demanded. "If you want your breakfast."

Butch cared more about the contents of the boat than his meal. Until his owner yelled one word: "Treat."

The panting and scratching halted almost immediately as Butch turned tail toward the house and rocketed back inside.

Was Trash Man still outside?

Crystal didn't dare move. Her question was answered a few seconds later when she heard a truck door open and then close. Almost immediately after, the engine roared to life. She exhaled and, for the first time, noticed how cold her fingers had become.

"I need warmth," she whispered to Brewer. "Like real warmth. A fireplace or, hell, I'd settle for a campfire at this point. My fingers are going numb."

She flexed and released her fists a couple of times. Was she being dramatic? Probably a little. Being hungry, tired, and cold had a way of giving her a flair for drama.

"I'll check it out," Brewer said with a smirk. "See if it's safe to slide out of here so we can go somewhere and eat."

"While you do that, I'll check my phone for a nearby diner or breakfast place," she supplied. Scrambled eggs and hash browns sounded amazing to her right now. Add a cup of coffee and she would believe she'd died and gone to heaven.

There were no messages from her siblings, even Duke, which she took as a good sign that things were stable at the hospital. The text from Elise requesting a phone call tightened the knot in her chest. A phone call generally meant bad news.

According to the map feature on her phone, a diner was a fifteen-minute walk from their current location.

"It's safe to exit," Brewer decided.

Crystal wasn't looking forward to getting out into the biting wind again. Winter had arrived at the same time as fall, lacing the wind with ice. They'd made it through the night unscathed and in one piece, which had been no small feat. This case was shaping up to be the most difficult of her career.

Challenge accepted.

Crystal could call her boss from the restroom of City

Diner on Avenue K. She wasn't looking forward to the walk, but she could do anything for fifteen minutes, including brave the cold.

Brewer slipped out of the tarp first and then stood guard while she followed. Both crouched down low. Beside the wheel of the late-model Jeep parked next to the boat sat a basket. A picnic-type basket. What the...?

He held her back with a protective hand. While she appreciated the gesture, she was here to protect him, so she stepped forward and scanned the street. Out of the corner of her eye, she caught a dark image in the window across the street.

Crystal turned her head to get a better look. The person immediately shifted out of view.

Before Butch caught on to the fact strangers were in his driveway, Crystal nudged the basket with the toe of her boot. She cringed, half expecting the thing to explode.

When it didn't, she crouched down and grabbed a stick. Using the end of the stick and keeping as much distance as possible, she flipped the basket open.

Food. There were breakfast bars, individually wrapped muffin packs, and two coffee-in-a-can drinks.

Brewer grabbed the basket handle as they stayed crouched behind the Jeep. It was only a matter of time before Butch came perusing the front windows or was let outside to do his business. The dog had a set of pipes that would wake the neighbors.

"We need to move," she whispered to Brewer before hitching a thumb toward Butch's house.

"I know," he said. "Should we return the basket to the old lady who's been watching us from behind the curtain across the street?"

"She's a senior citizen?"

"Afraid so," he informed.

"Then we weren't exactly stealth in our hiding place, were we?" She'd seen someone in the window but hadn't been able to make out the outline to determine male or female, let alone age.

Turned out Brewer had a superpower—exceptional eyesight.

He shook his head. "Although to be fair, the reason we didn't pick that side of the street was because the light was on inside the home."

"True," she agreed. "I need to return my boss's call, and I'm freezing out here. Let's return the basket sooner rather than later, okay?"

"We can do it right now," he said, crawling on all fours to the end of the driveway.

Crystal followed, then popped to her feet in a swift motion once she reached the sidewalk. She linked her arm in his and leaned into his warmth as they crossed the street.

The front door across the street cracked open.

"Eerie," Crystal said out loud.

Rapid-fire barks sounded as Butch charged the chain-link fence behind them. They'd narrowly escaped that one.

"Do you want to stay back?" Brewer asked Crystal.

"No," she immediately responded. "I have no plans to sit on the back burner while you take all the risks."

BREWER COULD RESPECT Crystal's decision. He respected her even more for it. To be fair, she was law enforcement and, therefore, used to taking risks. "I'm used to working with a familiar team," he said. "We know each other's moves almost better than our own."

"I won't do anything other than identify myself as a US

marshal to begin with," she stated. She had the badge and gun to back up the statement. That should help make this conversation go easier. The bigger question had to do with the older woman. "What do you think she wants from us?"

"People randomly bake food for me all the time," Crystal stated like it was common knowledge. "If you're not getting the same treatment, that's on you." She shot a soft elbow into his ribs.

He laughed, which made him cough. Sharp pain shot through his chest. He'd taken damage but would live. His shoulder where the bullet fragment had grazed could use some TLC to keep it from getting infected. He'd experienced that before while on a mission—almost lost his pinky finger because of it. So, no thanks on an infection festering. Best to nip it in the bud before it became an issue.

The open door sent a bad feeling rushing through him. It could've been muscle memory, though. The last time he'd walked through an opened door, he and his unit had been immediately bum-rushed by the enemy. Brewer had ended up with the pinky cut and Philly—because John Padulla was from Philadelphia—had left the scene with a gash in his shin so deep they could see bone. Not a pretty sight.

It had been a sure way to make Hanson Baker, comms guy, lose his lunch when Philly had pulled up his pant leg to reveal tissue and bone.

The other thought still lurking in the back of his mind was curiosity about what Crystal's boss had to say. After last night, maybe her SO was checking in to see if they were still alive. The bounty on his head complicated matters.

He stepped onto the wooden stairstep leading to a porch. The screen door was propped open, and the interior door was still cracked. What the hell were they about to walk into?

"It's open," a fragile-sounding voice said. "But you can leave the basket on the porch if it suits you better."

Brewer turned and locked gazes with Crystal, who had the same *no clue what's going on* look on her face. She reached inside her jacket, no doubt going for her service weapon just in case.

"Ma'am, my name is Marshal Remington," Crystal started.

"Oh?" came the confused voice.

"Who am I speaking with?" Crystal asked.

"Name's Dorothy," she replied. "The military man can bring anyone he pleases with him inside. I don't care too much for the law, but I can make an exception."

Crystal stepped into the door frame and then pushed open the door using her toe. "So, you don't mind if I enter your home?"

"Already said I don't," Dorothy pointed out. Brewer liked her candor, and there was something else he trusted about the older woman. There was something in her voice that said she could be trusted. His instincts had served him well...and they'd been on alert the day he'd lost his buddies and part of his leg.

Inside Dorothy's house was dark, and the place looked as expected. Vintage wood pieces in various states of wear and tear were covered in doilies and porcelain figurines that had, no doubt, been collected over a lifetime.

"Ma'am, thank you for allowing us inside your home," Brewer immediately stated as he stepped a foot in the door. Heavy flowery curtains covered the windows, keeping most of the light out. There were stacks of magazines and books everywhere—on the floor, on top of bureaus. This wasn't exactly at the level of *hoarder*, but it measured pretty close in Brewer's book.

"Well, close the door, or you'll let all the heat out," Dorothy quipped. The older woman had a full head of white hair cut short and brushed spiky. Although the style looked matted to one side of her head, so he wasn't certain the spiky part was on purpose. She sat, hands folded in her lap, wearing an almost ear-to-ear grin. She had on what could only be described as an old-school dressing gown complete with pockets that looked sewn on after the fact, socks, and fuzzy slippers.

Dorothy beamed up at Brewer.

"Thank you for your service," she said to him.

"You're welcome," he replied. Hearing those words never got old.

"My Joseph served," she continued before glancing around. "Where are my manners? Would you like something to drink? Coffee? Tea?" The older woman pressed a button that caused her recliner to push her to standing, easily.

"Something warm," Crystal said. "Coffee would be amazing."

"You can eat what's in the basket," Dorothy said with a smile. The fact she had several teeth missing didn't dim her smile. She reminded him of his aunt. Not in the physical sense, but attitude. You couldn't get much sassier than his aunt. He might have just found her match.

"There's no poison in there if that's what you're worried about. And I hate to burst your bubble, but there's no 'coke' in Coke anymore either—not like when I was young." Dorothy winked, and it caused Brewer to crack a smile. He couldn't help himself. She was feisty.

"I'd like coffee too, if it's not too much trouble," Brewer said, amused.

"Is there a place I can make a private call?" Crystal asked.

"Bathroom's over there," Dorothy said, pointing to the hallway.

All business, Crystal thanked her before crossing the living room. Her demeanor stressed him out if he was being honest.

He followed Dorothy into the kitchen, where she instructed him to sit at the eat-in table before getting to work on her Mr. Coffee machine. The old model vibrated and hissed as it filled the room with the aroma of fresh brew.

Dorothy inhaled. "Doc says I can't drink more than one cup a day. What does that bastard know?"

Brewer laughed. "You should probably listen to him. The world needs more Dorothys." He wanted to add *and less people trying to kill me*, but it would require explanations he didn't care to give. Being inside in the warm house was too good to pass up, and Dorothy's hospitality might end abruptly if he explained his situation.

"Take a muffin," she urged as she set a mug filled with coffee on the table in front of him. She motioned toward the basket.

"If you insist," he said, taking a blueberry one.

Brewer took his first sip of coffee as Crystal joined them. One look at her expression tied a knot in his chest. "What is it? What's wrong?"

Chapter Twelve

Crystal glanced at Dorothy and then back to Brewer. For a second, she wondered if it was a good idea to discuss what her boss had just told her in front of their host. On balance, she decided Brewer deserved to know. "Your friend is MIA." Keeping names out of the equation was for the best for all involved.

"What does that mean exactly?" Brewer asked, his gaze intensifying upon hearing the news.

"You know what it means," she stated. "He didn't show for work today and is no longer answering his cell."

A muscle in Brewer's jaw ticked. "We're going after him. We have to find him. He's in this mess because of me."

Crystal wasn't so sure, but Brewer's loyalty to his friend was admirable. "Absolutely not." Plus, she was pretty certain he had it backward.

She didn't want to discuss this further in front of Dorothy. She turned toward the elderly firecracker of a woman. "Thank you for your hospitality."

"Oh, where are my manners—please sit down," Dorothy said, motioning toward the chair opposite Brewer.

"We should probably get—"

"Don't be silly." Dorothy waved her off. "If you had somewhere to go you wouldn't have been sleeping out in the cold in Cranker's boat. If he'd have caught you, I'd be plugging up bullet holes too."

"How did you know where we were, by the way?"

"Got one of those Rings," Dorothy said with a smirk.

"I didn't see one on the door." Crystal had looked too.

"It goes anywhere. It's on a battery." The older woman's smirk widened. "I stick one on my camper out there, and it picks up what's happening on the road." She waved her hand like she was presenting her kitchen as a showpiece. "Don't have much here to steal unless someone wants to pawn old coffee mugs." She had quite the collection displayed in a box-type frame with enough cubbies for twenty or so cups hanging on the wall. "Got one from every state after my husband retired. Put my favorites up on the wall. We took to the road every summer." She put a hand over her heart as she spoke. "Those were good times."

"I'm sorry for your loss," Crystal said.

"Thank you." Dorothy fixed a cup of coffee for her. "Sugar? Milk?"

"A little milk if you have it," Crystal responded.

"Sit down and I'll get it."

She took a seat. "If it's not too much trouble."

"Nah, I don't get the pleasure of much company these days." Dorothy went to work, looking happy as a lark. "Don't get out much either."

Brewer had been quietly stewing. Plotting?

"Grab something to eat while I pour the milk." Dorothy started humming.

Crystal's toes finally thawed out. She wiggled them to make sure they still worked. Thankfully, they did. She took one of the muffin packets marked *Blueberry*, along with a banana. While she wrangled with the packaging—she would never understand why manufacturers made it so hard to open bottles and packages—Dorothy set a cup of coffee on the table.

The senior citizen glanced at the clock hanging on the wall. It was a black cat with big eyes. For every second that ticked by, the cat's eyes moved. "I better watch my show. If you'll excuse me. I like to watch it first thing and I'm days behind. Go ahead and eat while I'm in the next room."

The move was clearly meant to give them privacy.

Dorothy padded out of the kitchen and returned to her recliner. She clicked on the TV and turned up the volume to *80s boom-box blast* level. Again, was she giving them the opportunity to speak? If so, Dorothy was an angel.

Brewer took the package out of Crystal's hands and then ripped it open, using his teeth. He handed it back and leaned forward. "What happened to Trent?"

"That's what my boss is trying to find out," Crystal answered.

"I have to find him," he said.

"Not a good idea." She leaned in too. "Or do I have to remind you how dangerous it's been out there for us?"

"Doesn't matter." He shook his head. "He wouldn't leave me to rot either."

"Have you considered the possibility he's done that already?" Crystal regretted saying those words out loud the minute Brewer's face dropped. She was walking a tightrope here with her witness. Push too far and he would disappear and go rogue. "Look, I'm not saying that's what happened."

"Sounded like you were to me."

"I'm sorry if I offended you," she continued. "It's my job to consider every possible outcome."

"He's loyal."

"Possibly," she stated. "Either way, it's still my role to think outside the box."

"You don't know him."

"No." But she could say that she knew of him. She also knew he was being investigated due to his involvement with Crane in the first place. That wasn't what Brewer wanted to hear after finding out his friend had gone missing, though. He was under the impression that Trent was innocent in all this. Trent might've been. He might have been duped by someone he believed to be in legitimate business. He might have been helping a former associate down on his luck. "There is another possibility when it comes to Trent."

"Which is?"

"He went into hiding." It was plausible. "Your friend might have realized the hornet's nest that has been stirred up and decided to disappear until it blew over."

"I know where he would go," Brewer said after a thoughtful pause. "Hell, I'm pretty certain he told me exactly where to meet him."

"The place off the grid?" she asked after taking a bite of muffin. Questions were mounting, like whether or not the location would be compromised because Trent had been the one to give it to Brewer, but her growling stomach won out.

"Yes," he said.

"Where is that exactly?" She realized they'd gotten rid of his cell phone, which was where the information was stored.

"East Texas," he supplied.

"That's vague," she said.

"There was no map so I memorized the coordinates," he stated like that was a common thing to do. His military training served him well. It was also serving them both right now because Crystal was certain Dorothy's kindness had to do with his cargo pants and military-issue rucksack.

"Why doesn't that surprise me as much as it should?"

The depths of Brewer shouldn't shock her. Her physical reaction to him threw her off balance.

"Let me see your phone," he said before extending his hand.

Would he give her the wrong coordinates? Ditch her?

Time would tell. She had a feeling time was about to be up.

No doubt Trent was in over his head because of Brewer. He pulled up coordinates on Crystal's phone after she handed it to him, nabbed a screenshot before handing it back. Those coordinates were an hour south of Trent's location. She would be safe there.

In the meantime, could he lose Crystal?

After getting to know her, the thought of placing her in danger sat like a hot branding iron against the center of his chest. No one else would die because of him.

He handed back the phone. "That way you'll have the location in case we get separated."

Crystal eyed him. Based on her expression, she'd read between the lines. "Are you counting on that happening?"

"No," he defended. Too fast?

His answer was written all over her face. "I don't intend to let you out of my sight. So, I won't need these coordinates." She deleted the screenshot.

He had to give it to her, she'd caught him red-handed. "I'd feel more comfortable if you'd let me give you the coordinates."

The look she gave him could have shot daggers at him.

"We both know that will lead me off the trail." She paused long enough to take a sip of coffee. "My coffee hasn't had time to kick in yet, so I'm real cranky right now. For the sake of argument, let's pretend you didn't just try to pull the wool over my eyes. Okay?"

"Got it." More than ever, he was impressed with Crystal. No one had read his intentions so easily. The fact should've freaked him out more than it did. Crystal was unique, a one-off. She wasn't the norm, or he wouldn't have survived this long. He chalked up their connection to thinking along the same frequency and promised himself it wouldn't happen again.

The TV shut off, and the hum of the chair's motor in the adjacent room replaced it.

"I'll be darned if the one person who shouldn't win always seems to," Dorothy exclaimed from the next room. She padded into the kitchen and sized up the breakfast table. "Neither of you have eaten squat. Unless you're telling me you're not hungry or there's something wrong with my food, eat up."

"The muffins are amazing," Crystal said, turning her attention away from Brewer and toward their host.

"I have to admit, I assumed you were homeless," Dorothy said. "The way our military is treated after their service is inexcusable."

It made sense why she'd left the food basket now. Her husband had served. She'd had a ringside seat to the sacrifices that entailed. Hell, military wives deserved medals as much as their spouses. They brought up children as single parents until their husbands came home on leave and messed with the schedules. They acted as head of the household before stepping aside, in most cases, to give their husbands room to make decisions. And it worked the other way around too. Military husbands were just as deserving while their wives were away. The burden of running the house fell onto the parent at home. Being away, missing family was another issue. Brewer had seen that side and heard his buddies talking about it while on missions together or in the mess hall.

Military service wasn't always an easy life.

Being single had its benefits. Brewer didn't have anyone back home to answer to or miss for that matter. He didn't have to worry about whether or not his kids were listening to their mother since he didn't have those either.

His life was uncomplicated.

Was it lonely?

Brewer could admit to himself that the past year had felt like he was missing the boat. The feeling went against everything he'd convinced himself he prized. And he didn't buy into the whole *I need a relationship to complete me*.

Brewer was a complete, fully formed human. He glanced down at the metal shin underneath his pant leg. At least, he had been fully formed once. Now he felt more like patchwork, but that was a whole different mental slippery slope he didn't need to go down right now.

"Who wants a breakfast sandwich?" Dorothy's voice interrupted his thoughts.

"I don't want to eat you out of house and home," he countered, even though a sandwich sounded better than good to him. He'd trained himself to get by on very little food, to conserve when the situation called for it. He could survive on a couple of muffin packets. Being back on US soil, he'd gotten spoiled by having coffee every morning. Without it, he became a cranky pain in the neck. One of many signs he was getting weaker, not stronger. And another reason he didn't need to think about entering into any serious relationship. He'd come back broken. Who needed that in their life?

"It's no trouble." Dorothy eyed him up and down. "You'll need two."

Brewer cracked a smile. "Then, yes, ma'am."

He made a mental note to have groceries delivered to replenish her supplies. Her generosity was much appreciated. It was the very least he could do.

"How about you?" Dorothy asked Crystal. "Will you be having one or two?"

"One is good," Crystal said after thanking her. "Can I help?"

"No." Dorothy waved her off. "It'll give me something to do besides sit in front of the box." She referred to the TV. "Doc says I should exercise more."

"I'm not sure this counts," Crystal said with a laugh. "But we'll take it."

Seeing a light in Crystal's eyes was a powerful draw. She was even more beautiful when she smiled if that was possible.

Dorothy turned around and winked before getting to work on the sandwiches.

"We're being spoiled," Crystal said. "Would it be all right if I poured another cup of coffee?"

"Help yourself," Dorothy said, looking pleased with herself.

It dawned on Brewer why the woman might peek out her window or spy on others, help strangers. Everyone needed a purpose. Without purpose, it was easy to get lost like a boat in the sea during a hurricane.

Being in the military had given Brewer purpose until

the incident. He refused to call it an accident or blame it on bad intel. The incident had been his fault. He'd made widows out of two young women. Dorothy seemed to have had a long life with her husband before he passed. Hadn't the others deserved the same?

Because of him, several children would grow up without their fathers.

And now Trent was missing. He had a family. Had his wife and kid disappeared too?

Chapter Thirteen

Crystal polished off her sandwich in no time. She wasn't in a hurry to leave the relative safety of Dorothy's home. The US Marshals Service couldn't match this woman. Then there was her generosity. Crystal would make certain groceries showed up in the next day or two. Dorothy could be the millionaire next door for all Crystal knew, but she didn't live like she had anything more than a fixed income to get by on.

A spitfire in every sense of the word, Dorothy was the opposite of Gram Lacy. Lacy was the softest, kindest person Crystal had ever met. Grandpa Lor had a firm but kind way about him.

To be fair, he would have been happier if she'd stayed back and worked the paint-horse ranch, but Crystal had wanted to make her own way. Now none of her siblings or cousins truly knew how to run the business, and they might be faced with making decisions none were qualified to make. At least they had Shiloh Nash, the foreman, to lean on. He'd worked the ranch for decades. Based on age, he probably should have retired five to ten years ago. But the man was still strong as an ox and determined to "be useful to others," as he'd put it. Long ago, Grandpa Lor had given Nash the property he lived on along with the home he'd built. Most times, Nash stayed in the bunkhouse to be close to the horses. He had a reputation for being able to hear the horses' thoughts just by touching them.

Nash was like a favorite uncle to Crystal. She couldn't imagine Remington Paint Ranch without him working there.

Crystal shook off the mental fog as Dorothy set plates down in front of her and Brewer.

"Everything okay?" Brewer asked.

She looked up to realize he'd been studying her. "Yeah." The word came out despite the frog in her throat. "Sure. I was just thinking about my family's ranch, got lost for a few minutes."

"Have there been any updates?" He picked up the sandwich and took a bite before chewing.

"No," she admitted with a headshake. "I'm taking the no-news as a good sign."

Dorothy joined them at the table with a muffin and cup of yogurt. Her forehead wrinkled in concern.

"It's my grandparents," Crystal explained, figuring it couldn't hurt. "They were in a serious car crash and are in the hospital."

"I'm sorry," Dorothy said with a look that said she understood and sympathized. The pair of cobalt blues staring at her had seen loss. It was the kind of look Crystal imagined would be on either of her grandparent's faces if one lost the other.

"Thank you."

A rogue tear welled in Crystal's eye. She tucked her chin to her chest, turned her face, and coughed. Trying not to be conspicuous, she brought her hand up to wipe away the tear as more emotion welled up inside her.

What the hell was happening? Her tear ducts threatened to turn her into a faucet, which was the last thing she needed. Brewer was already questioning whether or not he wanted to stick with her for protection. Considering the dangerous near misses they'd had in less than twenty-four hours together, could she blame him?

"We should probably head out soon," Crystal finally said, rejoining the conversation. Brewer's plate was clean. She polished off the last few bites of her sandwich, chasing the food down with coffee that was warm on her throat and almost too good to be true.

"I hope everything works out all right for your family," Dorothy said with the kind of sincerity that brought another wave of emotion coursing through Crystal.

"I appreciate the good thoughts," she responded. Prayers, good thoughts, healing crystals…she didn't care what folks used for comfort. She was grateful for the sentiment all the same.

Dorothy nodded.

Crystal needed to get them out of there and to the white four-door sedan parked down the street, waiting for them by now. Her SO had supplied another vehicle after Crystal explained why she'd detoured from the roach motel plan.

With Brewer's cell phone gone, she figured they were going to be a whole lot luckier about not being followed or attacked every few hours. A new safe house had been set up in McKinney, which wasn't far. Elise was banking on the fact Crane's crew and the bounty hunters would bet Crystal would head south with Brewer. That or north to Oklahoma where there were plenty of fishing cabins dotting Lake Texoma. Staying near the area where they were last tracked should throw everyone off track. If they knew about the coordinates from Trent, it might be assumed they were fake to throw people off course.

At least, that was the logic. Fingers crossed. Crystal's plans hadn't exactly worked out so far.

They'd spent the night in the boat without being detected unless you count a harmless nosy neighbor. Dorothy wasn't actively trying to kill them, so that was a plus.

When the last drop of coffee was gone from Brewer's mug, he turned his attention toward Dorothy. "I can't thank you enough for your hospitality."

"You're more than welcome," Dorothy said, her voice surprisingly soft. She practically beamed at Brewer, her eyes filled with appreciation. In the sprinkling of photos around the cozy living room, her husband was young and in uniform. Dorothy's eyes filled with moisture. She blinked a couple of times. "You take care of each other, now."

"We're only together for a short time," Crystal immediately said, not wanting to give Dorothy the wrong impression of the relationship between herself and Brewer. Without being able to explain the reason life had paired them up, Crystal had nothing else to add. She bit down on her bottom lip to stop herself from overexplaining and inviting more questions.

"We promise," Brewer interjected. His answer was the one that seemed to satisfy Dorothy.

"Good," she said.

"What's the best way to leave here without being seen?" The last thing Crystal wanted to do was draw attention to Dorothy. If there were others in the neighborhood who liked to peek out their curtains and take notes on their neighbors' activities, she didn't want to give them a reason to get out their camera phones. Being stealthy and staying stealthy was becoming more and more difficult given new technologies. Crystal felt the need to add, "Or heard."

"Butch across the street is pretty active this time of day," Dorothy pointed out after a thoughtful pause. "He'll bark at his backside when he passes gas."

Crystal couldn't help but laugh at the image.

"These houses are front entry and the backyards, I'm guessing, are chain-link fence," Brewer added.

"That's right," Dorothy confirmed. "But you knew that from last night when you climbed into the boat."

"Folks look out for each other here?"

"That, or need something to gossip about," Dorothy stated with a cackle, clearly amusing herself. "If you climb out the window by the trailer, you should be able to wind around the other side of it and get on the sidewalk without anyone realizing this is where you came from." She caught Crystal's gaze. "That is what you're worried about, isn't it?"

Crystal nodded. No use trying to snow this lady.

"And they say you can't believe cop shows." Dorothy shook her head. "It's how I figured you for law enforcement."

"Guilty," Crystal said, not pointing out that she'd identified herself as a US marshal when they'd entered Dorothy's home a couple hours ago. "But I need you to forget we were here, okay?"

"Done," the woman said without fanfare. "Besides, who am I going to tell? My son moved to Colorado with his granola-eating girlfriend. Barely see them once a year at the holidays."

"It's important that you forget what we look like too," Crystal pointed out. "And maybe erase us from your Ring if you can."

Dorothy nodded.

"Thank you again for everything," Crystal said. She wasn't normally a hugger but gave Dorothy a hug anyway. They would've been a whole lot colder, hungrier, and crankier at this point if it hadn't been for Dorothy. Plus, who knew what else. Dead? "If anyone stops by asking if you've seen us, you haven't."

"I'm clear on what I need to do, and believe me, I can handle myself," Dorothy reassured.

Good. Because Crystal would never forgive herself if harm came to this sweet, albeit feisty, woman because of her actions.

"My advice is to cozy up to one another," Dorothy said. "Folks will look away." The move would have the added benefit of making their faces harder to be seen or recorded on more of those Ring devices.

Brewer stood up. He'd been too quiet for Crystal's liking.

"Will do, Dorothy," he said, taking a couple of steps toward the older woman. He bent down and planted a kiss on top of her head. "You're an angel."

Dorothy blushed. She shooed him away. "Go on now so I can forget I ever saw you."

Crystal knew how impossible it would be for her to forget Brewer. It was going to be hell once this witness was successfully delivered to trial. Because it would signal the end. And she wouldn't be able to wipe him from her mind like she'd done so many others before him.

A BATTLE RAGED inside Brewer's head. On the one hand, sticking with Crystal would give him more resources to work with. On the other, being with her put another good person at risk. And she was a good person. There was a long list of other things she was too, but this wasn't the time to go into how thoughtful or intelligent she was.

Crystal stood at the bedroom window. She stepped aside. "You first this time."

He limped over, thinking how much it would stink if his good ankle/leg stopped working properly. Then again, the other was made of metal, so he probably shouldn't worry too much. He opened the window, shaking off thoughts of what happened the last time they'd stood in a similar position. His shoulder still needed medical attention, but the longer they stuck around Dorothy's place, the more danger they brought to her doorstep. Bounty hunters wouldn't care a bit about murdering an elderly person to get what they really wanted…him.

Brewer climbed out the window, straddled it for a second to scope out the area, and then finished exiting. At this point, he could probably bolt and outrun Crystal. Or could he? His so-called good leg was giving him fits. It might be a sore joint, or he could have tweaked it. Then again, the cold front that had moved through went straight through his bones. It was probably just his imagination taking over, but he would swear the cold went right through his metal leg.

Being part metal, part man was going to take some getting used to.

"Hey," Crystal said as she climbed out the window. "Where did you go just now?"

"It's nothing," he said, embarrassed he'd lost focus even for a few seconds when he should've been vigilant about watching the area. His mistakes were piling up, costing lives, and risking safety. "I'm good."

Brewer refocused as Crystal moved to his side. He opened his jacket, figuring it would cover more of her that way. She'd lost track of her Stetson yesterday during the fight with the first bounty hunter, so neither had head coverings, which would have both provided a screen and warmth.

"It's even colder outside now," Crystal said, looping her arm inside his coat. Contact sent more of that electricity rocketing through him. "But if we wait ten minutes, the weather will change."

He didn't react to her attempt at humor. He couldn't let himself off the hook so easily. This time, he wouldn't allow any distractions. "Where are we headed, by the way?"

"Down the block," she said, palming her cell phone. The map feature was open, and there was a red blinking pin on the street behind them and down the block.

"Another vehicle?" he asked.

"White four-door sedan," she supplied.

"And another safe house?"

"That's right," she confirmed. "McKinney. In an area called Adriatica. It's a house this time, with a garage and small courtyard. It should be private."

"Sounds good," he said.

"I can't wait for a shower and change of clothes," she admitted as they turned the corner toward the vehicle.

Could he disappear while she was in the shower? He wouldn't leave her without a vehicle, so he'd have to figure something out there. With no cell phone, he couldn't exactly make a call. Not that he knew anyone around these parts who would drop everything and lend him a vehicle anyway.

He could hot-wire a motorcycle if he could find one. That might be an option. And while he was wishing, maybe there'd be a helmet and leather jacket too.

A thought almost stopped him cold. Crystal would try to find him. She would do her level best to hunt him down.

Would that bring more danger to her than if he brought her along with him?

It was a valid question. Would Elise reassign her if she lost her witness? Would she be able to take leave and go to the hospital to be with her family? Or would her file be marked from now on, considered a risk.

Once they got to the house, he could case the situation. Plan. Think. Figure out the right time to make a move. Because it was only a matter of time before he brought death to the marshal's doorstep, and her grandparents needed her.

Taking off would be for the best for everyone involved. No matter how much he tried to convince himself of that fact, the annoying voice in the back of his mind tried to argue.

Brewer could get himself to a trial date without help. More than that, he needed to prove to himself that he still could. When the time was right, he'd break off and find Trent.

Chapter Fourteen

The key was exactly where Elise had said it would be, sitting on top of the back tire on the driver's side. Crystal held the key fob on the flat of her palm. "Catch."

Brewer's reaction time was ridiculous. He caught the key with ease, like he'd expected the toss all along. His reflexes were finely tuned. The man didn't even blink.

"You drive," she said to him. The lack of communication from Duke about their grandparents was probably a good sign. Still, Crystal wanted to check in, and after a rough night in the boat, she selfishly wanted to shower and sleep the minute she and Brewer were in a secure location. The cold had a way of zapping her energy.

"You sure about that?" he asked.

"Yes," she confirmed. "Why?"

Brewer shrugged before unlocking the doors. As he put his rucksack in the back seat, he said, "Figured this was a government vehicle and that you'd have to drive for insurance purposes, or something like that."

Those were good points. "We're making up our own rules now."

It took two minutes to program the address into the car's navigation system. The drive to McKinney was a straight shot up US 75.

Once on the highway, Crystal informed Brewer that she needed to make a call. He knew enough about her situation for her not to feel like she needed to do so in private.

Duke answered on the second ring. "Crystal, hey."

"How's it going in Mesa Point?" she immediately asked.

"It's been calm since we last spoke," he responded, and she exhaled the breath she'd been holding.

"That's good, right?"

"Neither one has coded, which is a good sign," Duke explained with a hesitation in his voice she didn't like.

"What has you worried, Duke?"

"All of it, if I'm being honest." Her brother made a good point. "The fact that their recovery might take weeks or months if they recover at all. The fact that this in-between state could drag on, leaving them both in limbo. And then there's the unthinkable that could happen." He stopped right there. He didn't say that one of them could wake up only to realize their best friend and lifelong partner had died, leaving them all alone. Crystal and the others would ensure the survivor was well cared for and had plenty of company, but she couldn't imagine losing someone she'd loved her entire life.

She mentally shook off the possibility.

"I get it," she said. "I feel the exact same way."

Duke exhaled. "Didn't mean to unload on you like that, sis."

"You didn't say anything we aren't all thinking," she pointed out.

"How's your case going?"

"It's interesting." She couldn't say much else, and her brother of all people would understand why without needing an explanation. "Congratulations again to you and Audrey, by the way. The fact that you found each other almost makes me believe in love."

"We have you to thank," he said. "If you hadn't given me a heads-up that she might be in danger, I never would have stopped by her cabin that day to check on her."

"I'm just happy you caught the bastard in time," Crystal said. Audrey had been the target of a serial killer who'd cut the ponytails off female deputies after murdering them. The man was one twisted sonofabitch who was going to spend the rest of his life behind bars, where justice would be served for the families of the innocent victims he'd brutally killed.

"At least something good has come out of me being here," he said. "I feel like I'm failing our grandparents by not being able to do anything to help them recover."

"Being there is enough, Duke. You're helping Nash keep their livelihood going and making sure they have a business to wake up to. That paint-horse ranch is their life. They started it together and built it to what it is today. They poured their hearts and souls into that ranch. If you ask me, you're doing the most important work right now."

There was a long pause on the line.

"Thank you, sis. I needed to hear that today."

"I should be there with you," she said.

"If I don't get to feel guilty, you don't either," Duke countered. "We made an agreement to take turns, which we're all doing. Besides, physically being here isn't going to make them wake up or get better any faster."

He was right. She knew he was right. And yet guilt still sat heavy on her chest just the same. It wasn't just guilt for not being there today. It was a long history of guilt for not making it home for birthdays because of work. Then there was that one Christmas where no one had made it home. She remembered hearing the disappointment in Grandma Lacy's voice, disappointment her grandmother had tried to mask.

That had been last year. Possibly their last Christmas together.

Moisture gathered in Crystal's eyes.

"Sis?"

"I'm here," she said, hearing the frog in her own throat.

"It would be just like you to comfort me as you're headed down a slippery slope of guilt," Duke said with compassion. "Try not to, okay?"

He really knew her.

"I won't," she promised. "Everyone else good?"

"We're all rowing the same boat," he said. She understood what he meant.

Brewer turned onto Mediterranean Drive, where they were transported to the small Croatian village this area had been built to resemble. The house at the end of Seaside Lane would give them several possible exits should their location be compromised once again.

"Duke, I have to go."

"Take care of yourself, and we'll see you soon," her brother said. She'd read middle children were the peacemakers, negotiators. As tough and stubborn as Duke could be, he was also usually the one who brought reason into a heated situation.

"See you soon," she echoed before ending the call.

"Your brother?" Brewer asked. It was more statement than question.

"Yes," she said as he tapped a button and the garage door opened.

"Sounds like you guys have each other's backs." Brewer surprised her with the observation.

Then it dawned on her. He didn't have siblings. Who had his back?

"I WASN'T EAVESDROPPING on purpose," Brewer felt the need to point out.

"It's okay," Crystal said. "I wouldn't have made the call in this small space if I was concerned."

He nodded before pushing the button one more time to close the garage door behind them.

"I should probably go in first to check the place out, just in case," Crystal said.

"We're a team. Remember?"

There was no way he was letting her go in alone after everything they'd been through together. Plus, it wasn't like he could ditch her right now. She would make a phone call that would put a tail on him in two seconds flat. It might have been the reason she'd entered their destination into GPS, so her SO could keep tabs on them if something happened to Crystal's phone.

Brewer was taking no chances. He'd bide his time until it was safe to make his quiet exit. Trent was either in trouble or in hiding. The thought occurred to Brewer that if his friend was in trouble, he might have already given away the coordinates he'd shared with Brewer. There was no amount of torture that could persuade Brewer to turn on a friend, but everyone was different. Trent had a family, whereas Brewer had no idea what that might be like.

"Let's do this, then," Crystal said with a half smile that caused his chest to tighten.

She drew her weapon and headed toward the door into

the home. He located his and followed, sticking so close he might was well have been her shadow.

The three-bedroom home was impressive to say the least. The feel of the neighborhood transported him back to Europe during a couple of his furloughs. The cobblestone streets and Mediterranean flare made this area look like it had been here for centuries. In reality, it was all probably new builds from within the last five to ten years. He had to hand it to the developer, though. This area didn't feel like he was in Texas anymore.

The home was easily worth a million dollars. The place was done up to the nines with coffered ceilings. In the kitchen were white marble countertops with a gas range that had six burners plus a grill plate. The building itself was stone, along with a Mediterranean-style roof. The living room had a stone fireplace with a flat-screen mounted above the mantle. There were hand-scraped hardwood floors throughout with large windows. The courtyard, filled with flowers and plants, sat behind an iron gate.

"When can we move in?" he teased once they'd cleared the place.

"Right?" she answered, just as amazed as he was by the details. "I'm a country girl at heart, but I could make this place work." She smoothed the flat of her hand across the marble in the kitchen. "Too bad I'm not much of a cook. This would be wasted on me."

"What do you eat?" he asked, surprised there were people out there who didn't know their way around a kitchen. It wasn't a sexist thing either. It was a survival thing.

"I heat," she responded like he should've been doing the same. "The grocery store has a lot of precooked meals, and I don't have a lot of downtime. I eat on the road a fair amount. I've always wanted to learn but never made it beyond baking cookies during the holidays."

"That counts for something," he offered.

"They're the kind you break off from a roll," she said with a laugh that could brighten the darkest room. Or soul, he thought.

But that was a conversation for a different time.

"I know the heat works fine in here, but do you mind if I light the fireplace?" Crystal asked as he checked the fridge for food. He wasn't hungry but needed to assess the situation to see if they should go out at some point or have food delivered.

At least a week's worth of meals were in various restaurant to-go containers inside along with makings for sandwiches and breakfast. There was bread in the pantry. All right, then. This place was a go.

Crystal struck one of the oversize matches in a box next to the hearth and then turned the gas on. The fire lit immediately. Sure saved a whole lot of trouble cutting firewood, drying it out, and then using up half a newspaper as kindle. "Is it wrong that I want to take a shower and brush my teeth more than anything else right now?"

"No," he responded. While she showered, he might do the same, but not before checking all the window latches. "Does this place have an alarm?" He'd seen a box by the door to the garage.

"Yes," she said. "Matter of fact, it does." She rattled off the code to arm and disarm it. "I didn't want to set it until we got everything from the car."

He nodded.

Sneaking out while Crystal showered wouldn't give him enough time to figure out new transportation, so he would stick around until she fell asleep. Disarming the alarm might wake her if she was a light sleeper. But then, the main bedroom was upstairs, far away from the door to the garage.

"Take the main bath," he said to her.

"Are you sure?" she asked. "The shower in there could fit two people." She cleared her throat as she realized how that might sound. "I didn't mean us two or anything."

Brewer shouldn't be as amused as he was. "Didn't think you did."

He disappeared for a minute to grab his rucksack and an overnight bag that had been placed inside the trunk, locking the vehicle for good measure. Once back inside the house, he set the alarm, paying close attention to how loud the beeps were after arming it. Normally, the beeps lasted thirty seconds, enough time for the person who set the alarm to get out the door without triggering it. He counted. Yep. Thirty seconds. This was a standard system. It would be monitored, of course. The person who lived in a million-dollar home would take precautions.

"Here you go," he said, handing over Crystal's over-night bag.

She took it, not immediately budging from her spot on the hearth. "These fake logs might look pretty, but they sure don't give off a lot of heat. You have to sit right on top of them if you want to get warm." She studied him, asking a question with her eyes. Did she have to sit on him? Or was she sitting in a false sense of security?

Brewer wasn't a liar. He threw his hands out. "I'm here, aren't I?"

She smiled. Let her guard down a little? "Yes, you are."

Not providing the whole answer could be considered de-ception. Nothing had been black-and-white since leaving the military. In all honesty, there'd been gray area there too. Life in the civilian world was the gray area. But he wasn't an outright liar and it mattered to him she knew that about him before he took off.

Chapter Fifteen

A shower, a toothbrush, and clean clothes were better than Christmas morning as a seven-year-old.

Crystal finished dressing before checking the closet to find it full. Dresser drawers were the same. She located a fleece sweater and then put it on. After last night, she couldn't get warm enough. Unless the kiss she'd shared with Brewer stamped her thoughts. Then, all of a sudden, she was on fire.

She had to push that unprofessional thought aside and force her gaze to stay off those thick lips of his, lips that had covered her mouth and moved in a way that caused her stomach to freefall just thinking about it. How was that for keeping her cool?

At this point, it was dinnertime. The sun was descending, so she walked around and closed the blinds in all the upstairs rooms before heading back down.

Brewer was studying some fancy espresso-slash-coffee machine that was all chrome and stainless steel.

"Need a hand?" she asked.

"I probably don't need any more coffee," he said with a shrug. He'd showered and changed into low-slung jeans with no shirt. Her fingers itched to trace the muscles on his broad shoulders and back.

The shirtless image of him wasn't helping her tamp down the attraction.

"I can give it a try if you want," she offered.

He stepped aside and turned, leaning his hip on the marble countertop. Lucky marble. "One of us should figure out how to use this thing. You don't want to know me without my caffeine fix in the mornings."

The man was lethally gorgeous.

She cleared her throat and walked in front of him, bending down to study the machine. She'd seen something like this before when she'd protected a chef once. He'd been reluctant to leave home without his machine. People and their fancy coffee-slash-lattes. The brown liquid was a means to an end for her. Turned out, her tastes when it came to coffee weren't all that sophisticated. She could make instant work when she had to. It wasn't great, but it got the job done. "Let me see." She ran her finger along the back of the machine, found the On switch. Tapped it.

The machine came to life.

"How'd you do that?" Brewer asked, clearly impressed.

"Protected a chef once," she said. "He showed me the ropes on his machine. I figured these were probably all similar once you get over a certain price point."

Brewer didn't respond. He folded his arms over his chest and watched. Jealous?

No. There was no way Wade Brewer would be jealous of her protecting another man. Not to mention the fact Chef Gerard wouldn't measure up in any way, shape, or form to the former Army sergeant.

She located the well to put beans in. "I'm not sure if this is for espresso beans or regular coffee."

"Why don't we test it out, see what it makes?"

"Sounds like good teamwork to me," she stated, pleased with herself for getting them this far.

Her stomach picked that moment to remind her it was dinnertime. Loudly. It shouted at her.

"Or we can wait until after dinner," Brewer said.

She turned to face him, which ended up being a big mistake this close. Her fingers wanted to run their tips along the tattoo on his left shoulder and down his arm. Was it some kind of tribal tattoo?

"What sounds good?" he asked, stepping away to open the fridge door.

"If there was some form of pasta inside there, I wouldn't hate it," she stated. "And if it had seafood mixed in, even better." They were nowhere near the coast, but her stomach didn't know that.

"I have the answer to your prayers right here." Brewer held out a box from Sea Breeze Fish Market & Grill.

At this point, Crystal's mouth was practically watering. "I've heard of that place." She took a couple of steps to close the gap between them and took the offering. "There's enough inside here for two people if you're game."

"Tee up," he said by way of response. "What do you want to drink?"

"Water," she said. "We should probably both drink more of it. Best to stay hydrated."

She heated and plated their meals while he set the table rather than eat at the marble counter with bar chairs. "It's nice to have a sit-down meal tonight."

"Agreed," he said, "but I should put on a shirt."

"Don't bother," she said. She cleared her throat. "It's just us. You should be comfortable."

Considering he had on jeans and no shirt, it struck her as

odd that he had on socks. She remembered his injury and figured he must've been hiding his prosthetic. Was he embarrassed by it?

"I was giving my shoulder a chance to breathe," he said, glancing at the cut there.

Now she was embarrassed. She'd been so distracted by his hot bod that she'd complete forgotten about what had happened in the bathroom last night.

Had it really only been last night?

Time always seemed to slow in a case like this, and this one took the cake as far as danger was concerned. "There will be supplies here to take care of the injury on your shoulder. I'm decent at cleaning wounds if you'd like my help."

"I'll let it breathe for now," he said. "As long as you don't mind that I'm not wearing a shirt to dinner."

"No," she said quickly. Too quickly. She could feel her cheeks heat.

The food smelled amazing, so she picked up her fork and took a bite before she could stick her foot in her mouth again.

Plates were clear in a matter of minutes. Actually, they were more like bowl-plates and had been perfect for seafood pasta.

"I've got dishes," she said.

"You heated the food," he argued.

"Really, it was no trouble. I pushed a couple of buttons on the microwave." It was dark outside, and sleep tugged at the corners of her mind. "Plus, I need to figure out this fancy dishwashing machine before I head to bed." She almost added the word *alone* but stopped herself in time, saving herself at least that much embarrassment. Tonight

had been one for the books when it came to speaking before thinking. "What does your tattoo mean?"

"It's the mark of my unit, which essentially is my tribe,"
he said, examining his injury. "Only two of us are still alive.
One if Crane's men have their way."

"That's my job," she said. "I'm here to deliver you safely
to the courtroom."

"And then what?" he asked, surprising her with the question. He had to have thought of the consequences of testifying before now.

"Witness protection program, if you're interested," she
supplied, wondering how the suggestion would go over.

"I'm not worried about myself," he said quietly. "But
my aunt doesn't deserve to be targeted, and she will be.
Even after the trial."

"Normally, these bastards have short memories," she
said. "Once we put a leader in jail, the fight for who takes
his place is enough of a distraction. But in this case…"

"They want me dead," he supplied in a blunt manner.

"Badly," she said, hating the thought he would disappear
after the trial. WITSEC or no, Brewer would disappear. He
knew better than to show his face unless he had a death
wish. "You'll want guarantees for your aunt."

"Can she go into the program without me?" he asked.

"It doesn't really work that way," she said.

"I figured as much." His deep timbre took on a reflec-
tive quality. He was considering his options. She couldn't
blame him. "How successful is your program in keeping
folks alive after they've testified?"

"Of the ones who stay in? One hundred percent alive.
There are those who leave the program because they miss
loved ones or the old neighborhood. Those instances don't

usually end well. Once they leave the program, they leave our protection. There's nothing we can do because there isn't a budget to have marshals watching over individual homes twenty-four seven."

"Makes sense." He winced as he ran his finger along the cut that would leave a scar.

After loading the dishwasher, Crystal located a first-aid kit and rejoined Brewer in the kitchen. She opened the latch to find fairly extensive supplies. There was enough in there to stitch someone up, if needed.

"Mind if I take a look at your injury?" she asked, catching his gaze. The second their eyes locked, she knew she was in trouble. The pull toward Brewer was strong. Too strong.

Forcing herself to look away was her only hope at breaking the magnetic force.

"Go for it," he said after clearing his throat. The move gave her the impression that he struggled as much as she did when they stood too close to one another. The fact shouldn't have made her smile. It did anyway.

Crystal rummaged around in the tackle box–style kit. On the top level were antiseptic wipes. She would need those, so she pulled several packets out. And then there was a tube of antibiotic ointment. She would definitely need that.

She examined the cut, noticing the other scars on his chest, arms, and neck. "What happened here?" She ran her finger along a two-inch scar near the base of his neck running down his back.

"Gun fight," he said before clarifying. "A piece of shrapnel caught me above my body armor. The darn thing bled like you wouldn't believe. One of the folks in my unit turned white. Didn't think I would make it home." He laughed, which only caused his stomach muscles to flex. "Turned out to be a scratch."

"Looks like more than a scratch to me," Crystal said, thinking they could use up the rest of the evening talking about all the marks and scars on his body. Did he have half this many on his heart?

Forget the question. She didn't need to wonder about Wade Brewer's romantic life.

"It's nothing."

"Either way, I'm sorry this happened to you," she said, refocusing on the wound. When he didn't respond, she continued. "I'm going to clean the wound with an antiseptic wipe first. Okay?"

He mumbled an okay.

"I won't do anything without giving you a heads-up first."

"Good," he said. "I don't like surprises."

She figured that statement covered more than just this moment. Good to file away the piece of information. It made sense that someone in his former line of work who followed orders to a T and willingly went into hostile situations wouldn't like to be caught off guard. He had enough evidence on his body to prove he'd experienced more than his fair share of them.

Crystal ran her finger along a line on his tattoo.

"We designed our own," he said. "During one of our fireside late-night chats with too much time on our hands, we realized we all had Celtic blood running through us. So we decided right then and there the basis for the tattoo should represent Celtic tribes."

"That must be the knot here in the center," she said as she went about the work of cleaning his injury. Getting him to talk about the artwork on his arm was two-fold. First, it distracted him from the sting of cleaning the wound that was pink and angry. Second, she could learn a little bit more about him. Tattoos usually had a meaning behind them. It made sense when she really thought about it. If she was going to put permanent ink on her body, she would want it to mean something beyond the surface.

He craned his neck to look, and the scent of peppermint toothpaste filled her. Toothpaste had never been sexy in her book until now. Then again, anything would be sexy on this man.

This seemed like a good time to remind herself that he was dangerous too. And he wasn't exactly opening up to her. Even if they were in ideal circumstances and this was a romantic getaway instead of a safe house, he was a closed book.

"These kinds of tattoos have deep ties to nature and the elements of fire, water, earth, air, and space," he continued, sharing the most about himself that he had since they'd met. "Four of us were in a unit together, so we determined which element fit our personalities. The knot symbolizes life, death, and the afterlife too." He paused as though it was difficult to talk about this.

"We don't have to—"

"No," he said, cutting her off. "I want to. I never talk about the men in my unit, which is shame."

"Why not?" she asked as she applied antibiotic ointment to the deep gash.

"There hasn't been anyone I wanted to talk about them with," he said. Those words, his deep timbre, caused warmth to burn through her. "Philly disappeared once we came back stateside. My best guess is he's living off the grid somewhere, refusing to talk about what happened or the unfairness of the two of us still being alive."

"Thanks for trusting me," was all she said. All she could say.

"Talking to you is easy," he admitted, surprising her once again.

"Believe it or not, I never talk about my family life with someone I'm protecting," she said, figuring he deserved to know the feeling was mutual. "Opening up isn't my strong suit, so I'm told that I don't talk to most people. At least, that's what my last couple of boyfriends said when we were breaking up."

"They were fools to walk away from a woman like you," he said before catching himself.

"If it makes you feel any better, they didn't." Why was she sharing any of her personal life with Brewer? The lid was open—she might as well spill the drink. "I broke up with them. They, of course, pointed out that I'd kept my running shoes on from our first date."

"Then you've been dating the wrong type," he said. "Because I'd make sure they came off with everything else you were wearing if you were mine."

The possessiveness in his tone gave her the same sensations as the first drop on a big roller coaster. She had to stop herself from pointing out that that could never happen considering he was a witness in her care. He wasn't offering. Still, the comment caused her knees to go weak for a few seconds.

Crystal needed to change the subject while she still had control.

Chapter Sixteen

Brewer cleared his throat to ease some of the dryness.

"Do you want a bandage to protect the antibiotic ointment?" Crystal's voice broke through the mental image stamping his thoughts of her naked and the two of them tangled in the sheets. Her touch was tender as she worked on his injury. He could imagine those same hands gripping his body, fingers digging in so she could brace herself for the ultimate...

Glancing down at his prosthetic shin and foot, he couldn't imagine anyone would want him now. He clenched his teeth. "Sure."

Eyes forward, he forced himself to stop noticing the way her hands felt on his body. What good would it do to go down that road—a road that would only lead to heartache and pain? Pain of missing out. Pain of having no prospects. Pain of having a lonely future.

Pain of regret?

With the right mindset, Brewer could grind through anything. He'd made it this long. He could grind out the rest of life too with sacrifice and discipline.

"You got quiet on me again," Crystal said. She'd let her hair down and had taken on a more casual tone with him. Most likely, she was too tired to keep up the stiffer professional front. They'd been through a lot in the past day and a half. This was the point where folks started mentally breaking down.

This was the point where Brewer's training kicked in. He doubled down on shutting out emotion and hyper focused on the goal. This was the point where discipline kicked in.

"It's a training technique so I won't focus on the pain," he said, motioning toward his shoulder. A truer statement had never been made. It might not have been the same pain she thought he was talking about, but it was pain.

Crystal bit back a yawn. With a full stomach and a warm home, she wouldn't be able to fight exhaustion much longer. Once asleep—and he'd paid attention to her habits last night—he would be able to slip out.

She slept hardest when she first fell. Last night, she'd tossed and turned after about an hour, so he had a decent window to play with after she went down tonight. An hour, maybe. That would give him plenty of time to get his act together. His rucksack was already packed and ready to go. Nothing was stopping him from a quick exit when the time was right.

"Or we could talk," she said as she gingerly placed a patch on the wound. She then used medical tape to secure it.

"That's good work right there," he said, thinking he needed to grab some of the supplies and slip them into his rucksack before heading out. He was decently trained at field dressings and would need to stay on top of the injury.

"Thank you," she said with a self-satisfied smile. It tugged at his heartstrings, but he was determined not to allow it to change his mind about leaving. In fact, he was even more determined to keep her out of harm's way.

The niggling feeling he might end up hurting her career

with the move had him wanting to rethink his strategy. But he couldn't allow the thought to take hold. In the long run, she would be better off without him dragging her down. A small note in her file would be better than dying.

Everyone he cared about—and the list was small—was in danger or dead. He'd come home less than and was a cancer to everyone around him.

"I'm so tired my bones ache," Crystal admitted, taking a step back to admire her work. "But this looks good. I think you'll be able to save this arm." She shot a look of apology and then diverted her gaze.

It was common now and the reason he wore socks. He always kept his feet covered and wore long pants. Pants easily hid the area from beneath his knee to his ankle. He'd mistakenly put on running shorts to go for a jog out of habit when he'd first been cleared for exercise.

There were two types of folks in the world to him now— the ones who stared and the ones who couldn't look at him. Most fell into the second category, like Crystal right now.

Disappointment weighed heavy on his chest.

"You should go to bed," he stated.

Crystal hesitated before lifting her gaze to catch his. "I'm taking my work hat off with this next request." Her cheeks flushed and made her even more beautiful if that was possible.

He steadied himself for whatever might come next. "Go ahead. What do you want to ask?"

"For you to stay with me until I fall asleep," she admitted before quickly adding, "I'd totally understand if that's crossing a line for you and would respect your decision." She exhaled a long, slow breath. "With everything going on at home and the events of the last day and a half, I don't think I'd be able to relax enough to fall asleep without someone in the room with me." She paused. "Is that a strange request?"

He shook his head. "Not really." On some level, he understood needing comfort, reassurance after a near-death experience. Or in this case, a couple of them strung together.

"This place feels like a fortress in some ways, but..."

"In others it feels penetrable. Vulnerable." He finished her sentence for her.

"Yes," she said as her eyes brightened. Those beautiful eyes. He would say yes to pretty much any request if he stared into those long enough.

Being her comfort made him feel...useful again. For the first time in a long time, he felt needed. There was something primal about still feeling like he could protect someone. And about her asking him to be the one to do it. The fact that she felt safe with him caused a little bit of pride—and hope?—to sneak in.

"We can curl up on the couch if you'd like," she offered. "Might feel less personal that way."

He thought about how that might mess with his plans. "You'll sleep better in a real bed after last night."

"That's probably true," she admitted. "You know, this is bigger than last night and yesterday morning. My whole world tilted on its axis after my grandparents' accident. It's like the ground is shifting underneath my feet and I can't do anything to stop it."

He glanced down at his leg. "Believe me when I say that I know exactly what you mean."

"Right. Sorry. Of course you do. You've been through hell and back—and then got a job. I'd imagine you were putting your life back together after what must have been the absolute worst possible thing that could have happened to you and your unit. Only to find out you're working for a criminal." She paused. "I know I've said it before, but most people wouldn't do the right thing. They would cash in their losses with Crane and do their best to forget they ever worked for him."

"What would that solve?" he asked. "Crane would still be out there, shifting the ground underneath even more people's feet. I would still end up in hiding for the rest of my life. And nothing would be gained for the sacrifice."

"It's still honorable, Wade."

Was this the first time she'd used his first name? Somehow, it made those words strike a little harder, a little deeper in his chest.

"Well, I had and still have a lot to make up for," he finally said. Before she could say anything else that might make him want to stick around, he stood up. "We should get ready for bed."

CRYSTAL MIGHT'VE BEEN misreading Brewer, but she figured the minute she fell asleep he'd be gone. It was the reason for the request. Or maybe that was the lie she told herself— because she'd never crossed a professional boundary before.

Either way, keeping him close would alert her if he tried to slip out of bed. Generally, she was a light sleeper. Her plan should work, especially if she stayed awake until he fell asleep. Could she? She made no promises. She would fight sleep as long as she could before giving in and hope for the best.

Brewer not agreeing to curl up on the couch had her concerned. She would've been able to hear the alarm if disarmed from there. The move to give her the main bedroom—the farthest one from the garage door—wasn't lost on her. This wasn't her first rodeo.

After brushing her teeth, she met Brewer in the bedroom. Sleeping in her current outfit would be fine sans the sweatshirt. Shrugging out of it, her T-shirt rode up. Quickly, she dropped a hand to hold it in place and not give a peep show. Without a bra, she would be bearing all.

There might not have been much of a show, but her dignity was still intact as she dropped the sweatshirt onto the chair in the corner and then slid underneath the covers. The bed was bigger than any king she'd ever slept on. Must've been a custom job. Of course, it would be. Everything about this safe house screamed *custom* and *expensive*. Her SO had set them up well. Crystal reminded herself not to get too used to these kinds of digs. These places were rare and normally a favor being called in.

They were 0–2 when it came to safe houses, hoping to improve the numbers with this one.

Brewer changed into sweatpants, no shirt. The thought of being skin to bare-naked skin with that chest sent sensual shivers racing over her body. Warmth spread over her and through her as she met him in the middle of the oversize bed.

"I need to ask where this bed came from," Brewer said with a smile that tugged at her heartstrings. Too bad he was most likely plotting his exit. "It's the most comfortable thing I've slept on in ages. Then again, that's not difficult considering what I have to compare it with."

"Tents and hard dirt are most definitely the opposite of sleeping on a cloud," she said on a laugh, trying to break up the sudden tension in her chest. Her gaze dropped to his lips again. She couldn't regret the move, but it definitely wasn't helping stem the almost overwhelming pull of attraction.

"True," he said, his voice low and sexier than any man's should be.

"Is it okay if I get closer like last night?" she asked, not wanting to overstep her bounds. Last night, the boat had forced them to be crushed together and the cold had made being as close as possible an even better idea. Tonight was a different story. They had heat. They had room.

She'd had to make being close about something else. Since she made a terrible liar and had never acquired the taste for it, unlike her father, she'd gone with the closest thing to the truth. Everything she'd said had been from the heart. Her world was upside down, spinning out of control fast.

Brewer was a tether to reality. So, yes, she needed him and had been honest in every way that counted aside from the plea being a strategic move.

"Go ahead," he said, turning onto his back.

She moved into the crook of his arm and then he looped his arm around her, pulling her closer. His spicy male scent filled her senses, bringing awareness to every intake of air. His body was silk over steel. There was an intensity about Brewer that put ideas in her mind about how incredible he would be if they gave in to attraction and had sex. A voice in the back of her head reminded her it would be a bad idea. Not just for professional reasons, although that was a big one. But because he would raise the bar for sex. For what she should expect in the bedroom and, she suspected, out of it too, based on the way he'd treated her so far.

Crystal realized there was more to her attraction than circumstances. Brewer was intelligent, intense, honorable.

He had a smokin' hot bod that made her hands ache to roam all over it.

"Thank you for doing this, by the way," she said to him, attempting to guide her thoughts back onto a professional track and the real reason she'd asked for this. Being able to track his movement should he decide to bolt made suffering through a physical ache to be with this man in the biblical sense worth it.

"No problem," he said, but his gruff voice gave him away. A trill of awareness shot through Crystal along with a small sense of triumph at the fact he seemed just as affected.

A one-way attraction this intense would feel awful. Not that she would act on a mutual one.

"I forgot to mention earlier with the kind of day it's been," she started, realizing she'd neglected to share one of the most important pieces of information to him after receiving a text from her SO while showering. "The trial date has been set for Monday."

"Today's Friday," he immediately said.

"That's right," she agreed. "We only have to stay alive through the weekend, and I have to get you safely to the courthouse. Come Tuesday or Wednesday of next week, you and your aunt will be able to put all this behind you."

Based on how quiet he'd gotten, she had no idea if this information was good or bad. For the case, it was positive because it gave Crane's men less time to find and kill Brewer. She would be able to get to the hospital sooner rather than later, which was also a plus.

After spending time alone with Brewer, she needed to go home and hit the reset button. Not once in her professional career had she been tempted to cross the line with a witness. Zero. Granted, she had no intention of this being the first, no matter how much her heart protested.

"Good," Brewer said. "You'll finally be rid of me, and I can't make any more mistakes that could get us both killed."

"You? Mistakes?" she asked, shocked. "What's my excuse? You turned your original phone in but I should have taken your phone the minute I realized you had a second one."

"It's blown to smithereens now," he said as a quiet settled over Brewer. Intensity practically radiated from him. Nothing was going to get through.

They were both tired. They needed sleep. They would have a better perspective in the morning.

Crystal repositioned, moving her leg next to his. He immediately moved his out of reach. Had she struck a nerve?

Silence hovered like a thick cloud. Crystal fought the urge to give in to sleep. Something told her the news she'd just delivered made Brewer even more resolved to leave. Was she overreacting?

Ten minutes in, fighting to keep her eyes open, it finally happened. Brewer's breathing slowed to a steady, even pace. She could hear his strong heartbeat as she let go and drifted off to sleep.

Chapter Seventeen

The sun peeked through the slats on the blinds as Brewer blinked his eyes open. He immediately noticed the bed was cold where Crystal had been.

Had he nodded off? Slept the entire night? Dammit.

So much for slipping out while Crystal slept. He also realized it was the first time he'd trusted someone enough to sleep in their presence in a long time.

Tossing aside the covers, he threw on a shirt and headed toward the bathroom. Not five minutes later, he followed the smell of coffee to the kitchen. The clock on the wall said it was seven forty-five.

"Good morning," Crystal said with a smile in her voice. She had on a long T-shirt that fell to midthigh and not much else.

The fireplace was going, and the heat was on in more than one sense of the word.

"Hey," he responded, still trying to process the fact he'd fallen asleep. "I can't believe I slept the whole way through." He hadn't had a true night's sleep since the incident if he was being honest. After, there'd been nightmares. Then, waking up with phantom pain in part of a leg that was no longer there. That had been fun.

Crystal crossed the kitchen and went for a robe she'd

hung on the back of one of the bar chairs. She shrugged it on and tied the cinch to the point he wasn't certain she'd be able to breathe. "I didn't hear you coming downstairs."

Good to know he could still pull off being stealthy when necessary. "Didn't mean to catch you off guard."

"Not a problem," she said before crossing the kitchen. "I figured out the machine. What'll you have? I can do coffee, but that's boring. I can do a latte and I can do a cappuccino. Or the machine can, rather. I know what buttons to push, though, so that makes me the boss."

There was a spring in her step he hadn't noticed until now. Then again, their situation hadn't exactly called for lightness up to this point. And yes, it was great they'd had a real bed to sleep in last night in a million-dollar home. Who wouldn't be happy?

Happiness was fleeting. Brewer had learned the lesson firsthand. Would he ever be truly happy?

It was probably surviving a life-and-death situation together and being in close proximity that had him believing he and Crystal could make a life together.

Whoa there! Slow down, Brewer.

"Coffee with a shot of espresso works, if you can manage." His imagination was getting the best of him. Because they weren't a real couple and this situation was temporary. The fact that he was going to testify on Monday put his aunt and Trent in even more danger.

As it was, Brewer had no idea what was going on outside the bubble of this million-dollar home.

"I just had the same myself," she said with a satisfied smile.

He walked over to the fridge and started rummaging,

opting for a bowl of cereal. "Have you heard anything else from your SO today?"

"Nothing," she said as the machine hissed and groaned while it spit out brown liquid. "You like yours black, right?"

"Yes, ma'am," he said, realizing how military he just sounded. Force of habit.

"It's too early to be so formal," she teased before producing a mug that almost smelled better than she had last night. He could still remember the lavender scent that had filled him up and reached deep inside him, reminding him of fields of fresh flowers and the reason he thought this country had been worth putting his life on the line to protect.

"Sorry," he said, taking the offering. He inhaled a breath and ended up with more of Crystal's lavender soap in his body.

"Don't be," she said before grabbing her own mug. She lifted it up in a toast. "To us both waking up here today."

The way her voice slightly caught on the word *here* had him wondering if she'd figured out his plan last night. And then the reason she'd wanted to sleep together dawned on him. She was onto his plan. Or at the very least, she feared he would pull a stunt like the one he planned. Since they were way past being coy, he asked, "How did you know?"

"I didn't," she admitted. "I suspected."

He studied her for a long moment before shaking his head and grabbing his cereal bowl.

"I can make something better than that if you'd like," she offered.

"Thought you couldn't cook," he reminded her. Had she been playing him then too?

"Does breakfast count?" she asked. "I can do a mean

avocado toast, which technically involves a toaster, not an oven or stovetop."

"Do you cook an egg?"

"You got me on that one," she admitted, joining him at the table.

"Then you lied to me before," he said with more heat than intended.

"I didn't," she said. "I wouldn't." Catching his gaze, she added, "I couldn't do that to you. Plus, I'm a terrible liar."

It was probably his ego that wanted the statement to be true.

"Are you saying you've never had to lie in the course of doing your job?" he pressed, knowing he should probably quit while he was ahead.

"Is that what we're really talking about here?" she countered.

Brewer laughed and put a hand up in defeat. "Touché."

"Guess it's my turn to apologize."

"Never apologize to me for being honest," he said. The world had become too comfortable with lies as far as he was concerned. He'd heard plenty while rehabbing after surgery. Some folks might've called it optimism. The doctors and nurses had been full of it, telling him that he could still live a full life despite his permanent damage. They'd said it was up to him and that he could get the rest of his mobility back. As for the loss of hearing in the right ear, there wasn't anything that could be done there, but he was supposed to be thankful for hearing on the left side.

His frustration wasn't due to throwing a pity party for himself. The hand he'd been dealt was punishment he deserved.

"Okay, then," she started. Suddenly, the rim of her coffee

mug became very interesting. "Since we're being honest. Why did you pull away from me last night?"

"I didn't," he defended. At least, he didn't remember it.

"My leg touched yours," she continued without missing a beat. "It was innocent on my part, but you couldn't move away fast enough."

"You were on my left side," he explained, surprised when her eyebrow shot up in confusion. "My bad leg."

Crystal sat there for a long moment. Her expression revealed the moment she made the connection. "Your 'bad' leg. You don't like anyone to touch it?"

He nodded.

"Or see it," she continued.

It was time to change the subject, but he filled his mouth with a bite of cereal instead.

"Is that why you always wear socks?" She dropped her gaze again, not making eye contact.

"Trust me, you don't want to see my feet." Or should he say foot?

"It wouldn't bother me one way or the other."

"That's what you say now because I haven't taken my sock off," he pressed. Which person would she be? Someone who stared? Or someone who refused to look?

"Why don't you take it off right now?" Crystal probably shouldn't continue down this line with Brewer. As it was, he'd shifted in his seat three times.

"Because I'm eating."

"Then let me do it." Crystal caught his gaze. "What's the harm?"

She wanted to see his leg and his foot—not out of some morbid curiosity, but it occurred to her that he was hiding them. He was ashamed or embarrassed, which burned her to no end. The man had fought for his country. He'd been in battle. In her book, that made him a hero. And heroes shouldn't have to be ashamed of their body parts for being missing or broken.

Brewer's gaze intensified, almost daring her.

"Not without your permission," she clarified.

"You won't look at me the same."

"How about allowing me the opportunity to prove you wrong." It broke her heart that he thought he had to hide parts of himself from her, from the world.

"If I wanted this to become awkward, I would have taken my sock off already," he snapped.

Her body reacted to those words similar to a physical slap. "I wouldn't… I couldn't." And then it dawned on her that others might have. "It's okay, Brewer. Never mind." Crystal didn't easily accept defeat, except that she knew when she'd lost a battle, and there was no use beating her head against a wall.

Brewer set his spoon inside the bowl. He bent down and rolled up the jeans he'd changed into, stopping just above the knee. Next, he peeled off the sock.

"How does it work?" she asked. "When you have shoes and pants on, I can't tell a thing."

"That's the idea," he said. "A Texas-based company donated the materials. This works off muscles the same way the real thing would."

"It's kind of cool looking," she said. "Like the stuff superheroes are made from."

"You've seen too many Marvel movies," he said as a smile played with the corners of his mouth.

"You're still the sexiest man I've ever seen wearing jeans

and not much else," she said, then immediately realized she'd said the words out loud instead of inside her head as usual.

The look on her face after the slip must have amused him because his full lips broke into a wide smile over straight white teeth.

"Okay, I didn't mean it like in the unprofessional way," she quickly countered, rolling her eyes. "And don't let your head swell so big you can't make it out the door when we get the signal to leave."

"I'm a hot-air balloon at this point for how much my head is swelling," he teased. This time, there was a sparkle in his normally too-serious eyes that she hadn't seen before. It was nice, and she wondered if this was what he'd been like before the incident that had taken part of his leg. "We lift off after breakfast."

Crystal laughed.

Despite everything, it was funny. And it was good to laugh. There'd been too little laughter in her life up to this point.

"Eat your cereal, and then we'll talk." Based on his reactions so far, she was dead-on about him trying to sneak out last night. It was only Saturday. How on earth would she keep an eye on him twenty-four seven until Monday morning?

Glancing at the clock, she had roughly forty-eight hours to cover between now and then. Could she stay awake? Not go to the bathroom?

Okay, the bathroom part was pretty extreme. Could she get him to stay put might've been a better question. This home might've just been their ticket to staying alive until he needed to testify. Favors had been called in to get on the docket Monday.

He reached down to unroll his jeans.

"You don't have to do that for me, by the way," she said.

His eyebrow shot up.

"Cover up," she clarified. "I don't care one way or the other."

He looked at her like she couldn't possibly mean that. It dawned on her that he wasn't used to being treated like he used to be. He should've been. But she'd protected a witness who had a little girl in a wheelchair from cerebral palsy. The witness had said the worst part was how no one ever looked his beautiful little girl in the eyes or said hello. No one spoke to her in the grocery line or when he took her out in the park. It was the bit that broke his heart because his little girl deserved to be seen. She deserved to have people say good-morning to her when he dropped her off at school instead of the blank straight-ahead stares she got.

"You're the same person to me, Brewer."

He was almost fully hovered over his cereal bowl at this point, face down. When he looked up, he had a smirk on his face a mile long. "Still as hot?"

Again, Crystal laughed.

"Yep," she quipped. "Same level of hotness."

"Good," was all he said, but she heard so much relief in that one word it caused her heart to break a little more for him.

He polished off two bowls of cereal after rolling his jeans leg down. He kept the sock off, which she appreciated. She'd seen all the physical scars on his body from his time in the service, feared she'd only seen the tip of the iceberg when it came to the ones on the inside.

Brewer needed to know he was still gorgeous, hot beyond her wildest imagination, and…whole.

Was there any way to convey that to him in a way that could help him see it was true?

Crystal gave herself a mental headshake. She had to keep him alive until he could testify on Monday. Beyond that, professionally speaking, it wasn't her job to care what happened to Wade Brewer.

So, why wasn't she able to let it go?

Chapter Eighteen

Brewer glanced down at the metal foot as light bounced off what should have been the top of his arch. Superhero?

No. Bulletproof?

No. Special?

No.

He shouldn't get a medal for surviving when it should have been him behind the wheel that day. Today, though, he couldn't afford to jump on that hamster wheel of shame and guilt. Because he had a chance to save another friend's life. In order to accomplish the task, he needed to focus and put all distractions behind him. Which included Crystal.

Right now, he wanted to stay with her more than anything. Not because of the words she'd said a few minutes ago. He genuinely liked being with her. At the table, he'd laughed for the first time in a year. Probably longer than that if he was being truly honest. He'd joked. That wasn't something he was used to doing anymore either.

For a few seconds, Brewer had felt like himself again. As much as he wanted to hold on to that feeling a little while longer, Trent could end up dead. Not having contact with the outside world to know what was going on was driving him to the brink.

Leaving her was going to be one of the hardest things

he'd ever done. She would resent him for ditching her. She was also onto him. She was watching. He had to bide his time and find the right moment to make his exit. All he could do at this point was wait.

Crystal's cell buzzed. She retrieved it and answered the call.

"Hey, boss, what's going on?" She sounded surprised to get the phone call, which got Brewer's attention. "I see." She hesitated before finally swinging her gaze around to meet his. "Okay." She paused a beat. "No. Don't do that. There's no need." Another pause. "Seriously. I'm good. We're good." A final pause. "I'll let you know if anything changes. Thanks for the information." She ended the call.

"What's going on?" he asked.

"Damon has been sighted in the Dallas area," Crystal informed.

"Which means he's on the hunt for me." Brewer wasn't sure if he should take that as a good sign for Trent or not. It would be useful to know if his friend had gone into hiding or had been abducted. "Did your SO say anything about Trent?"

Crystal shook her head. "My SO would have said something if she had new information. She did, however, mention sending a replacement for me."

"No," he argued. "Absolutely not. I don't trust anyone else to get the job done. It's you or no one."

"I talked her out of it for now," she said. "But she wants to send him anyway."

"Why?"

"Said something about this assignment being bigger than one person and that it might be easier if we were able to take shifts so one of us could sleep," she continued.

"You told her not to do that," he confirmed.

"That's right." Crystal issued a sharp sigh. "This is a high-profile case. It's not uncommon to assign two marshals when we have the resources."

"But you don't," he interjected. "Do you?"

"Not really," she admitted. "I have history with the marshal she wants to send. History that is no one's business but ours."

"Why do I get the sense he's trying to get himself assigned to this case to get back on your good side?" Brewer didn't like that one bit. He didn't have a right to feel one way or the other when it came to her personal life. The kiss they'd shared, as electric as it had been, wasn't personal. Okay, he could admit it had felt personal in the moment, but there had been a tactical reason for it too.

"You would be correct."

"Has he been trying to contact you since we've been here?" he asked.

"Yes," she admitted. "But I haven't been responding. I do my best not to introduce my personal life into my work. The exception, of course, being with my grandparents. Mahone is crossing a line here."

Brewer studied her for a long moment. "Your SO doesn't know about your history with Mahone, does she?"

"No," Crystal said. "I think she suspects something, but when we first got together, we worked different districts, and he got himself transferred to mine after the breakup."

"Sounds persistent." Brewer's whole body shouldn't have tensed at hearing this even though it did. In the back of his mind, he was trying to work out the threat level now that they knew Damon was near.

While holed up in the million-dollar home, Brewer as-

sumed the threat was low, but it was dangerous to underesti-
mate Damon. The rival to Crane's organization was Michael
Mylett. Based on the intel Brewer had gathered while working for Crane, Mylett wanted to take over. Could Brewer
go to Mylett and spill more "company" secrets? Help him
take command of Crane's men in exchange for protection
for Trent and his family, Aunt Rosemary, and himself? He
would only bargain to keep himself alive so he could take
care of his aunt in her later years. Abandoning her to live
out the last years alone was wrong. He couldn't do that
after she'd welcomed him into her home and protected him.

Mylett hung out in Austin at the Roasted Bean. He considered himself a true businessman. Apparently he woke
at five forty-five every morning to go to the gym. After
a workout, he stopped off at the Roasted Bean, where he
sometimes met with his associates over breakfast. His office, much like Crane's, was the back of a blacked-out SUV.

His home would be a fortress. Not to mention the fact
Mylett might have Brewer shot for betraying his former
boss.

Brewer reserved this option as a last resort. At this point,
he needed information. He needed to know where Trent
was and if he was hiding or captured. He thought about
his aunt. Should he have her moved? Was it safe for her to
stay in the same place for very long?

Now that he'd tucked her away, he didn't want to dis-
turb her any more than necessary. She'd trusted him when
he'd asked her not to question why she'd needed to move
temporarily. She'd been able to take her cat, Tiny, with her.
Tiny, the twenty-pound cat who'd outgrown his name, had
sealed the deal.

"Talk to me, Brewer."

"There's not much to say." He tried to sell the line but couldn't. He couldn't sell what he didn't believe himself. He put a hand up. "Okay, there's a lot to say, but I don't know where to start."

"Then throw anything at me, and I'll do my best to answer."

"What about Aunt Rosemary? Is she safe where she is? Being targeted? Left alone? Should she be moved to another location for preemptive purposes?"

"I can take care of that." Crystal made a note on her phone. "What else?"

"What did you just do?"

"Put in a request to have her moved as I'm capturing your concerns," she said. "That might be something as simple as asking for a wellness check or extra local manpower to patrol your aunt's new location. Or alerting my superior so she can track down resources just in case." She looked up at him and blinked. "I'm on your side, Brewer. Or haven't you noticed that already?"

"You're doing your job," he pointed out. "This is my life we're talking about. I don't punch out and go home when this is over. Or have you forgotten?"

Those words landed with the equivalence of a physical punch. Crystal drew back and sucked in a breath.

Brewer felt like a real jerk.

"Maybe you're right about me," Crystal started, wondering where she should begin in defense of what he'd just said. "Maybe I do get to 'clock out,' as you put it, at the end of the day and go home. Last I checked, I was here with you trying to keep us both alive. Oh, and that's not all. I just got off the phone with my SO, who wants me to 'clock out,' but

I refused because protecting a witness is personal for me and I don't walk away just because a case is high profile or classified as the most dangerous of my career. I'm not here for my own health or to get some kind of gold star in my file. I'm here to protect you." She was starting to get heated. Emotion was overtaking logic. But since she was already strapped to this runaway train moving at full blast, she continued. "And do you know why I'm still here against my SO's better judgment?"

Brewer folded his arms across his chest and gave a slight headshake.

"Because I don't walk away from a witness who needs me."

"I need you?" he asked. His gaze narrowed and his lips thinned.

"That's right, Brewer. Believe it or not, you need me," she stated with more of that heat in her tone.

"Why is that?"

"Because no one is going to care about you and Aunt Rosemary as much as I do," she continued. "This is personal for me because I've gotten to know a little bit about you in the past forty-eight plus hours, and guess what? I like you. Despite the fact you look ready to walk out that door the minute I turn my back, I actually think what you're doing is noble. I think you're an honorable human being, and not just because you came home from a war you didn't start with battle scars."

"Then why?" His face was stone, giving away none of his emotions.

"Because you've been to hell and back, which could have turned you into a bitter jerk," she continued, spilling the truth like water from a fountain. "You're intense—don't get me wrong. You're not easy to get along with all the time. But you're strong, and I don't just mean in the physical sense. You're the kind of person kids need in their lives to have someone to look up to."

"More of that superhero nonsense."

"Maybe," she said. "But there aren't nearly enough people left in this world who are worth of looking up to, and you're one of them." She threw her hands in the air. If he couldn't see it at this point, she would never be able to convince him with words.

As she stood there, fuming, Brewer broke into a wide smile.

"What about being hot? You forgot to add my hotness to your list of good qualities," he said.

She wanted to wipe the smirk from his face. "You're also infuriating!"

"So, where do we stand on the hotness scale?" he continued, unfazed by the fact she was a teapot about to boil over. "Am I a nine or ten?"

"Jerk. How about that scale? Because right now I'd definitely say you're a ten." She cut across the room and tapped his good shoulder. He captured her wrist. "Quick. I'd give you a nine on the quickness scale."

Against her better judgment, she locked gazes with him. The moment their eyes connected, lightning struck. Was her heart in trouble? Hard yes. Was there anything she planned to do about it? Harder no.

The air in the room crackled with electricity. The heat between them could be a furnace for all of downtown Dallas. The only thing she could do under the circumstances was take a step back and drop her hand in order to break his grip.

She had no doubt he could have tightened his hold, but

he seemed to know this was a bad idea as much as she did. "I need air."

Without looking back, she disarmed the alarm and then walked into the garage, welcoming the cold on her heated skin.

She could think clearly in here, away from Brewer.

It was only a matter of time before he made his move. Should she have allowed Elise to send Mahone to double up on keeping watch over—and on!—Brewer?

His main concerns seemed to be around the safety of his aunt and his friend. There wasn't much she could do about Trent, considering she had no idea where he was and hadn't gotten back definitive intel as to which side he was on.

Having Brewer's aunt moved should ease some of his concerns. If Crystal was in control of his aunt's situation, that would also give Brewer extra incentive to stick around.

They had…she checked the time on her cell…forty-four hours to get through before she needed to safely deliver him to the courtroom. Had Brewer figured out this assignment only got trickier from here? That the danger increased dramatically the closer they physically got to the courthouse?

Should she prepare him?

Crystal reminded herself to get a grip. This was Wade Brewer she was thinking about. The man was former military. He would have thought through all the possibilities, assessed the risks by this point.

Was that the reason he wanted to ditch her? She could see in his eyes that he did. It was in the words he wasn't choosing to say.

The man had a unique ability to get under her skin. He could throw her off balance by existing in the same room with her. She might not have experienced anything like this before with a witness, or anyone else for that matter, but that didn't mean she wouldn't find a workaround.

Brewer wasn't the only one good with strategy and tactics.

A noise inside the house made her heart leap into her throat. He wouldn't be climbing out a window right now... would he?

Chapter Nineteen

Brewer bent down to pick up the dish he'd dropped while emptying the dishwasher. The plate had broken into four big chunks and more tiny pieces than he cared to count.

Crystal came rushing into the room from the garage. "Everything all right in here?"

"Peachy," he said, not bothering to hide his frustration. "It slipped right out of my fingers." He issued a sharp sigh. Was this another sign his body was no longer listening to him?

"It happens," Crystal said, checking the pantry before joining him with a broom and dustpan. She held them out. "I'll leave you to your work."

"You're not helping?" he asked, surprised.

"You can't clean up by yourself?" she asked, turning over the items.

"I didn't say that," he said a little defensively.

"Good," she quipped. "I figured you weren't helpless."

He didn't know whether to hate her or revere her for the fact she refused to help. On the one hand, it meant she believed he was fully capable of cleaning up his own mess. The operative words being *fully capable.* Even Aunt Rosemary had wanted to baby him after the incident. She hadn't offended him on purpose, but he'd been prickly as hell. The more she'd wanted to do for him, the less of a human he'd felt. So, he'd left after a few days, checked into a nearby motel—if it could be called that—and figured out how to fix his own meals. The dollar menu at the fast-food place within walking distance had been a lifesaver during his recovery.

Aunt Rosemary had insisted she go with him to his rehab appointments, so he'd been stuck in the back seat of a hot off-duty fireman's vehicle next to his aunt. He'd had to hear his aunt flirt with said hot off-duty fireman. It had been the only time that plan had backfired on him.

Brewer decided he respected Crystal for not helping. She was telling him that he didn't need it.

He would take Crystal's actions as a compliment.

Leaving her was getting more difficult by the minute. Say, for argument's sake, he did find a way to slip out. Where would he go? What would he do?

He had cash stashed in his rucksack, so he could pay for items without leaving a trail. That fact didn't help much when it came to ordering a car service. Those needed an app. Without a phone, his options were limited.

He picked up the broken pieces of the plate and set the four large pieces on the countertop. With the right glue, he could probably piece this thing back together again. Using broom and dustpan, he collected the smaller pieces. "Have you seen any glue around?"

"Glue?" Crystal echoed in a surprised voice like he'd just asked her to marry him. She didn't need to worry about that one even though she was exactly the kind of person he could see himself settling down with for the long haul.

"Turn up your hearing aid," he quipped. Teasing her was a lot more entertaining than it should be.

She joined him in the kitchen. "Why would I know where glue is? Does it look like I live here?"

"You should," he said. "Live here. This place suits you."

Crystal couldn't shake her head fast enough. "I'm a country girl through and through. Did you see how close the neighbors are?" She made a dramatic show of shivering. "Way too close for comfort."

"What are you trying to hide?" he continued, enjoying the momentary break in tension.

"What's gotten into you, Brewer?" She eyed him with amusement.

"Cabin fever?"

"We haven't been here a full twenty-four hours yet," she said with an eye roll.

"What can I say?" He threw his hands out wide. At least he had both of those and they still worked properly. Most of the time anyway. "I'm an outdoor person."

Crystal's laugh was the cliché. It was angels singing to Brewer's good ear.

He finished cleaning up the mess as she checked drawers.

"Everyone has to have a junk drawer in the kitchen, right?" she asked when she was coming up empty.

"Apparently people who live in million-dollar homes keep their drawers organized." Pretty much all of his kitchen drawers fell under the category of junk drawers. No wonder he hadn't made his first million yet—he didn't know the drawer trick.

Everything in this house had a place. Glue would be no different. "What about the garage?" he asked. "Did you see a toolbox in there?"

"I'll go check," she said.

He hadn't been paying attention when they'd first arrived yesterday and had yet to go out there today. In fact, when she came back inside, they should probably arm the alarm. He wasn't kidding about staying inside. On their initial tour, he'd seen a workout room. Could he get a good sweat going in there? Work off some of the tension building inside him?

The gym had been a lifesaver during his recovery. Even more so now. Weights didn't care who lifted them. The gym was equal opportunity. A private gym would stop others from sneaking looks through the mirror when they thought he couldn't see what they were doing.

But first, could he piece this plate back together?

Crystal returned, beaming. A small tube sat on the palm of her hand. "Beast Glue."

"Only the best," he said with a smile.

"Can you imagine yourself living in a place like this?" she asked. "Seriously?"

"No." He didn't have to think about his answer. "I wouldn't be happy. There's way too much concrete for my liking outside the door. Speaking of which, we should arm the alarm."

"Oh, right," she said, moving to the pad and then punching in the magic numbers that started the beeps. They momentarily took him back to hearing a similar sound in the hospital when he'd woken after the incident. The shock of glancing down to find he only had one foot. Then the slow process of being able to sit up again on his own. Patience wasn't exactly his middle name.

He pushed to be able to do more, against medical advice. What did doctors know about him? They knew generalities. They were schooled in what the average person could expect. They had no idea what would go down for each individual. Despite all the years in school and the experience in the field, it turned out that medicine wasn't an exact science.

Then came the tests, the fittings, the recovery. The learning to live with a new reality. The rest, as they say, was history.

He took the glue and fitted the pieces back together as best he could. "It's not perfect, but it's better than nothing."

Crystal studied the patchwork. "It's better than before."

"How so?"

"It used to be a plate just like all the others in the cabinet," she surmised. "Now it's an art piece."

Brewer glanced down at his body, wishing the same could be true.

CRYSTAL WALKED TO the living room and then plopped down onto the couch. She picked up the remote control and pressed a large green button. A cabinet opened above the fireplace, revealing a massive flat-screen. "Whoa."

It was Saturday, which meant college football.

"Do you want to watch a game?" she asked, figuring him for the football-watching type. She hoped the distraction would buy some time.

"I'm going to hit the gym," he said. "The door will be open if you want to work out together."

The invitation caught her off guard. She stretched out her arms and then legs. "I'll be there in a few minutes."

Fifteen minutes later, she pushed off the couch, having flipped through the channels and found nothing worth settling on despite having more options than she knew what to do with. The term *choice paralysis* applied here. More than not, trying to find a movie to watch at home took longer than actually watching a movie. By the time she found one, it was time for bed.

In the gym, beads of sweat rolled down Brewer's neck to pecs that bulged against his cotton T-shirt.

Crystal shook her head as she moved to a treadmill. This home gym was something. The room had a circular shape with a flat wall of mirrors. There was a treadmill, rowing machine, elliptical, and weight bench. There were various weights to choose from along with a few resistance bands. A couple of rolled-up yoga mats were tucked inside a basket, making it look almost like a floral arrangement. And, of course, there was another flat-screen TV mounted on the mirrored wall. She was half-surprised the room didn't have one of those exercise bikes that had been all the rage a couple of years ago.

Crystal located the remote and flipped to a music station that was the perfect for a workout. She glanced over at Brewer to see if her choice was okay, got a thumbs-up. Hard rock wasn't something she normally listened to, but it worked when she needed to get her blood moving either for a run or a workout.

Being a marshal meant passing annual fitness tests as well as shooting tests. She always had to be ready to fire her weapon when chasing dangerous felons or protecting a witness. This job wasn't like a suburban beat cop who might fire a weapon once or twice during their entire career. As a marshal, she had to fire frequently on assignment when she chased felons who had nothing to lose. Once caught and convicted, they weren't likely to step outside a prison gate for the rest of their life.

Those kinds of perps were notorious for shooting first,

asking questions later. And running. They liked running. Not in the going-for-a-friendly-jog sense. They were more in the vein of running-for-your-life runners. The boost of adrenaline that came with being so close to arrest gave them a superpower.

So, yes, Crystal trained. She hit the gym. She worked out.

Because she always had to be ready to catch someone on an adrenaline- or drug-fueled high.

An hour ticked by before they took a break. Of course, a million-dollar home would have a water cooler with cups like at the gym. She grabbed one for herself, then one for Brewer and filled both before handing his over.

"This was a good idea, Brewer."

"Always helps to get a good sweat going," he said through heaves. He looked around. "Who keeps fresh towels in their home gym?"

"Not anyone I know," she said. "But then we're all backyard-barbecue-and-beer type folks. This is a champagne-and-caviar lifestyle and definitely not a typical safe house. Someone important must live here."

He smiled as he wiped sweat from his face and neck. "Sounds awful, but then I don't eat raw fish either."

"You don't eat sushi?" she asked.

"Nope," he informed. "I like my food cooked all the way through." He made a face. "Too much bacteria otherwise."

"I'll take my dry chicken any day over single-celled organisms."

"Someone paid attention during biology class," he teased.

"A-plus student right here," she bragged.

"So, what's next?" he said to her when his breathing calmed down to a normal pace.

"We go to court," she said. "I thought you were in on the plan."

"I can't risk Trent's life," he stated.

"My SO is doing a little more digging into his background," she said, then held up a hand to stop him from going off. "Before you say anything or tell me what a great guy Trent is—and that might be true, by the way—at least listen."

Brewer shifted his gaze up and to the corner of the door frame before giving a slight nod for her to continue.

"We wouldn't be doing our job if we didn't investigate the man who put you in this position," she explained.

"You said something similar before," he pointed out.

"I meant it then too." Crystal took a sip of water. "Trust me?" She practically held her breath waiting to see how he would answer.

Chapter Twenty

"Fine," Brewer said to Crystal. "For the record, I believe in Trent. He wouldn't put me in this position on purpose."

"How can you be so certain?" she asked.

"Because we're part of a brotherhood that none of us would betray." The answer was just that simple. "We made a commitment to each other and our country. Those commitments create an unbreakable bond."

"Ever hear the name David Berkowitz?" she asked.

"Yes."

"How about Jeffrey Dahmer?" she continued.

"Of course," he replied. Where was she going with this?

"Dennis Rader?"

"He was BTK," Brewer responded. "What do these men have to do with Trent?"

"They all served in the military," she said. "And then became predators in the very country they swore to protect."

"That's not Trent," he argued.

"The list goes on," she said. "Serving in the military doesn't make him innocent."

Brewer shook his head. "Doesn't make him guilty either."

"Some people leave the military with scars you can see, like you," she gingerly pointed out. "For others, those scars aren't so visible." She paused. "You don't know which kind

Trent picked up or what might have been going on in the back of his mind before."

Arguing would do no good and she'd made one helluva point, so Brewer bit his tongue. Was he being naive when it came to Trent? Did he know the man as well as he believed he did? "Do what you need to do."

"Thank you for understanding." She wiped more sweat from her neck. "Even if I know you don't agree."

"I need to grab a shower," he said as she walked out of the room. With Crystal, he feared he might agree to pretty much anything she said. Brewer was convinced Trent wouldn't walk away if the situation was reversed. She hadn't heard Trent's voice on the phone like he had. She hadn't heard the regret or his apologies or the way he'd blamed himself and taken full responsibility. She didn't know how much Trent wanted to help Brewer get out of the situation he was in *because* of him.

A cold shower helped clear Brewer's mind.

The time was nearing when he needed to make his escape. Leaving tonight gave him time to get to east Texas and the spot Trent had practically said he'd be hiding. Brewer stood at the window in the upstairs spare bedroom where he'd placed his rucksack, staring out. This area of Adriatica Village housed villas. There were apartment buildings too—plenty of them. Which meant he should be able to find a motorcycle to hot-wire.

A plan was taking shape. If he was lucky, there'd be a helmet with the motorcycle. There was no hiding his rucksack. It was the one thing that could give him away. Then again, a motorcycle would get him to the destination off the grid much quicker than most cars, especially with the speed limits in Texas. *Limits* was a loose interpretation.

Drivers took the term *limit* more as a suggestion or a start-ing point than a limit per se.

If he disappeared, though, what would that do to Crys-tal's career? Would losing a witness put a mark on her file?

Could he do that to her after everything she'd done for him? After he'd told her more about his past than anyone else?

Brewer rejoined Crystal in the kitchen in time for a late lunch. They heated a Tex-Mex favorite—fish tacos. Sit-ting across the table from her, he wondered if finding Trent would go a lot smoother if he let her in on his plan rather than go behind her back?

After getting to know her, walking away was less ap-pealing. Plus, he didn't want to be the reason she got a mark on her file.

"I think I know where we can find Trent," he admitted. "If he's hiding, that is."

She cocked her head to one side. "The coordinates you gave me were fake, weren't they?"

Not much got past the marshal.

He shook his head. "They were close but far enough away that I doubted you'd hit the target." He still held on to the idea that he could go to Mylett if everything fell apart.

"Why put me in the area at all?" she asked.

"Because it was more believable that way," he admitted. "Then there's the fact I can't lie to you."

"I hope, for your sake, Trent is clean," she said. "I need to get approval from my SO before heading out."

"Does that mean we're going?"

"Only if I get the green light," she informed. "Other-wise, I'd be putting my career on the line to find someone who might be guilty as sin."

"If Trent is hiding, this is where he'll be," Brewer said. "I owe it to him."

"What if he set you up?" she asked. "Do you still owe him?"

"We'll cross that bridge when we come to it." Until proven otherwise, Brewer had to give Trent the benefit of the doubt.

Crystal issued a sharp sigh as she picked up her phone. "Here goes nothing."

LEAVING THE PROTECTION of the current safe house would be considered unprofessional if there was no threat. In truth, Damon was in Dallas and she'd received a text saying he was last seen on the train heading north. He was tracking them, and it was only a matter of time before he found them.

Which brought Crystal to her next point. They should've been heading south to Austin, where the trial was set to take place. Except that might be exactly what Damon would be thinking. She might be able to sell her SO on the fact they needed to do something unexpected if she was going to deliver her witness in one piece.

Going off the grid would be a hard sell, but Crystal would promise to check in frequently. Would her promise be enough?

Elise picked up on the first ring. "Give me good news."

Crystal argued her case before rattling off the coordinates. To Elise's credit, she listened quietly before making any judgments.

"It's a risk," she finally said.

"What isn't?" Crystal pointed out. "We stay here, Damon might find us in a matter of hours. We leave, we could get caught. My witness has a location that is unexpected. I think the risk is worth taking."

The rattle sound was most like Elise picking up the bottle of Tums on her desk and shaking it. The habit meant she was thinking hard.

"Do what you need to in order to keep your witness safe, Remington. I'd send backup if we weren't so short staffed." Elise was quiet for a beat. "Get him to court alive. I don't need to remind you how important this case is for our district."

"You can count on me," she promised, not liking the fact she was being asked to re-avow.

The phone was silent for a long moment.

"I have information coming in," Elise warned. "Hold tight."

Crystal didn't like the sound of this. She waved a hand to get Brewer's attention while he was putting away dishes and reloading the dishwasher. One look at her expression and he abandoned the job he'd been doing, immediately switching gears to erasing their presence. She didn't normally work with a witness who could hold their own. It was a nice change of pace.

Before Elise was back, he made a beeline for the stairs.

"My bag is in the bedroom, and I have a few toiletries in the bathroom," she said, covering the receiver with her free hand.

"Got it," he said before disappearing a moment later.

"You there?" Elise asked, coming back to the conversation.

"I'm here," Crystal confirmed.

"I've just received word Damon is in Adriatic Village," Elise informed. "You have to move. Now!"

Crystal immediately ended the call and jumped into action. By the time she reached the bottom of the stairs, Brewer was already coming down them. He'd shouldered his rucksack and had her bag in hand. "Damon's here."

"Go," he said, not wanting to waste a second.

She turned, grabbed her purse, and fished out the keys as she bolted toward the alarm pad. She punched in the numbers. A burst of adrenaline caused her hands to shake, but she kept it to a minimum as she grabbed the door handle.

In the next few seconds, she was behind the wheel, all thought of Brewer driving flew out the window as he hit the button that opened the garage door.

Crystal feared Damon might be standing on the other side of the door as it lifted, AR15 or some other rapid-fire weapon in hand, finger on the trigger.

It was too soon to revel in relief when the coast appeared to be clear. Damon was on the property, hunting them like a skilled hunter stalking prey. Lack of a phone to trace had bought them time, just not enough for her liking.

"You know what he looks like," she said to Brewer.

"Yes, ma'am," he responded, kicking into full-on military mode. He dropped his hand inside his rucksack and pulled out a Glock, keeping it low as he bent forward as if doing something as simple as tying a shoelace. The man wasn't breaking a sweat.

Staying calm under pressure saved lives. Considering the skill level of the folks they were up against, she needed Brewer's assistance if they were going to survive.

Rather than gun it and draw unwanted attention, Crystal navigated around the empty pathway out of the villas and into the restaurant and apartment area of the village after entering the small roundabout with a waterfall in the center.

Brewer casually surveyed the area, but there was nothing relaxed about the intensity of his gaze. Crystal worked the rearview and side mirrors, keeping vigilant watch to ensure no one seemed too interested in them. At this point in the afternoon, people stood outside a popular restaurant and more vehicles were on the internal streets.

Her best hope was to blend in.

Slowly, she made her way to the exit of the village, hooked a right-hand turn toward the highway. So far, so good. She'd learned a long time ago not to get comfortable too fast.

On Virginia Parkway, traffic thickened. It was another good sign.

Crystal navigated onto the highway without a tail. "It's too early to celebrate, but I need you to program in the ultimate destination or, at the very least, start talking. I don't have more than a vague idea of where we're headed."

"Maybe it's for the best if we take it one step at a time," he said. Didn't those words send an icy chill racing up her spine.

Did he trust her?

The reason dawned on her a few seconds later. If Damon caught up and captured her, she wouldn't be able to give him more than a general direction. Brewer was operating on military philosophy—need-to-know basis.

It was smart but also left the door open for him to lose her if they made a stop for gas or took a bathroom break.

Disappointment sat heavy on her chest at the thought that he didn't trust her after everything they'd been through together. After how much of their personal lives they'd shared. Hell, after working out together. She'd mistakenly believed they'd formed a bond.

Way to stay neutral on her witness.

Brewer was a special case. There were depths to him that were rare in an individual. From the minute they'd first met, she'd wanted to know more about him.

This seemed like a good time to remind herself that he'd been planning his escape all this time. He might've had depths that interested her, but that didn't mean he would let her inside. He was used to relying on himself and seemed to prefer it that way.

Still, it was difficult not to be impressed by the man. Their attraction burned. And a growing piece of her wanted to know how that would play out if it was allowed to run its course. After boyfriends like Mahone, she had a feeling Brewer would blow her mind, reach parts of her that she never knew existed.

And then what?

Walk away? Leave her heart shattered into a thousand flecks of dust?

On second thought, keeping a safe emotional distance made far more sense.

Step by step, Brewer provided directions moments before an exit needed to be taken. After just shy of two hours on the road, he told her to find a good place to hide the vehicle and park.

"There aren't exactly parking lots around here," she said.

"You're going to have to take this vehicle off road," he pointed out.

And get stuck? Break the only vehicle they had for a quick getaway? No thanks.

"Is there a plan B?" she asked.

"On second thought, we need to circle back and grab a few supplies from the gas station," he said. "Water, for one."

Had this been his plan all along? Get her out here in the boonies and then ditch her at the gas station?

Crystal was about to find out.

Chapter Twenty-One

"This might be the last real restroom you see for hours, possibly all night. Might be a good time to take care of business." Brewer fully intended to use the facilities.

Crystal shot him a wary look. He immediately caught the meaning. Telling her that he had no intention of ditching her wouldn't do any good. She needed to see it. So, he skipped the part where he would try to convince her. It would be a waste of breath anyway.

Brewer headed to the bathroom while she stood in the aisle. Waiting?

It dawned on him they'd come full circle with bathrooms. This time, he didn't have a phone or the intention of sneaking away. A small wave of disappointment that she didn't trust his word tried to take hold in his chest.

What reason had he given her to believe him?

Brewer washed his hands and pushed those thoughts out of his mind. They had a hike through maple, oaks, and river birch ahead of them, not to mention a person to find. After exiting the restroom, Brewer was surprised that he didn't see Crystal anywhere. A moment of panic struck like lightning on a clear day.

He grabbed half a dozen bottles of water and cleared out the power bars before heading to the cashier. On the way, he glanced out the window to realize Crystal waited in the car. Maybe she trusted him after all? Or maybe she had no choice.

After paying, he placed the supplies inside his rucksack and then headed toward her. As he neared, he realized she was on the phone. More bad news about them being followed? He picked up the pace.

She glanced up and nodded. A good sign?

Brewer opened the passenger door after placing his rucksack in the back. He eased onto the seat as she finished up the call. "Everything okay?"

"I called to let my brother know I might be out of range for a couple of days," she supplied.

"Once we find Trent, we can head to your hometown," he offered, not liking the wrinkle in her forehead. The crease was deep, meaning she was concerned more than she wanted to admit.

"Can't," she said. "Wouldn't be professional of me to bring a witness to the hospital on a personal errand."

Why did those words hit the center of his chest like bullet fragments?

"I understand," he said, needing to kick the relationship back to a professional level. Logic said they'd only known each other a matter of days. His heart argued it was already too late. He'd met enough of the wrong people to realize who the right ones were by this point in his life. Right people, wrong time? They wouldn't get a chance to know each other before he had to disappear for a couple of years, maybe more. A woman like her wouldn't wait. She would move on. The thought shouldn't strike like a physical blow. It did. "We should head out and find a good spot to stash the car."

"Right," she said, her tone all business as she gripped the steering wheel. She dropped one hand long enough to fish out her cell and hand it over. "Lead the way."

Brewer opened the map feature and studied it. "Head out this way." He pointed as he continued to focus on the map.

"All right, then," she said with no enthusiasm in her tone. "Time to get this party started."

Was she regretting putting her life on the line for someone like him? A broken-down soldier?

Either way, they were off to the races.

After finding a suitable place to hide the car, Brewer exited the vehicle and shouldered his rucksack. He noticed a couple of bags in the floorboard filled with water and packaged food.

"I have water and power bars," he supplied.

"Then we'll leave these here so we have something to come back to," Crystal said. "I got a text while we were back at the station. Michael Mylett's eighteen-year-old son was picked up on felony charges."

"What the hell for?" Brewer asked. He'd been betting on being able to go to Mylett as a backup plan should this one blow up in his face. How else would he keep Aunt Rosemary safe? The government?

"Aggravated assault," she supplied. "Looks like the kid will do time if the charge sticks."

Mylett would be in no mood to dole out favors if his kid was looking at prison. Time to pivot once again. Brewer was running out of options. He didn't have a whole lot of faith in one entity. He'd planned on stacking the deck.

After the trial, he could grab Aunt Rosemary and disappear. He knew how to stay off the grid. But his aunt? Now that he thought about it, she needed medication. She had her doctors in Galveston. Sure, leaving for a couple of days or a week was fine.

But months? A year? Two?

How would he make certain she could see her doctors in confidence, have access to her diabetes medication? There was no amount of hot firemen that could solve every issue. If Brewer went into hiding without her, they would use her to draw him out eventually.

Attachments left him vulnerable and hurt anyone who cared about him. At least Crystal would be safe once this was over. No one would come after her once Brewer was out of her protection. The only reason she was in danger now was because she could end up caught in the crossfire. No one would target her specifically. In fact, he'd noticed folks were going out of their way to isolate him in their attacks.

Crystal checked her cell phone. "I'm officially out of range."

Being off the grid had its uses. Although pointing that out to her right now when she had grandparents lying in the hospital fighting for their lives didn't seem like the right play.

"I apologize," he said to her, stopping long enough to look her in the eyes. It would be dark soon and they would have to move slower toward the spot, but this was important and he wanted her to know how he felt. "I'll get us out of here and back into cell coverage as soon as humanly possible. I know how important your phone is to you right now, and I hate being the cause of you needing to be out of touch in case your family needs you."

"None of this is your fault, Brewer." She folded her arms across her chest and studied him. "Is that why you think

I'm tense? Because I blame you for what's happening?" Before he could answer she added, "I don't, by the way. I'm a grown woman. I have a job that causes me to take risks."

Then, he was confused.

"I'm on edge because I half expect you to ditch me at any moment and it frustrates me to no end because I won't be able to find you," she explained on an exhale. "I will have disconnected from family to end up lost in these woods with no witness to show for it."

"If I gave you my word, would you believe me?" he asked, caught off guard at her reasoning.

"Yes," she said. That one word caused his chest to squeeze. It was important to him that she trusted him.

"I'll get us both out of these woods alive," he said. "That's a promise."

"Together?"

"Yes," he confirmed. "Together. I'm not leaving you, Crystal." He realized his mistake the minute her first name rolled off his tongue. He shouldn't use a familiar name with the marshal. He'd already crossed too many lines as it was. He needed to find a way to maintain a safe distance. Being personal wasn't the way to do it.

"Okay, Wade." Hearing his name roll of her tongue lit a dozen campfires inside him.

He vowed to do whatever it took to ensure he kept his promise.

SEALING THE DEAL with a kiss would be unprofessional, so Crystal wouldn't request it no matter how much her heart protested. She'd been concerned Brewer would ditch her and disappear, leaving her out here to fend for herself. Granted, she was a country woman at heart and she had a weapon, along with a backup. She'd strapped on her ankle holster while waiting in the car at the gas station.

"We better get to it before all the sunlight is gone," she said with a little more confidence this time. Having his word meant something to her. It touched her in a deep place. Now they just needed to stay alive so she could deliver him in one piece come Monday morning.

In a surprise move, Brewer reached for her hand and then gave a reassuring squeeze. The small touch provided so much relief. They were still a team—a team that worked well together. Good.

He let go, turned, and led her deeper into the trees. She couldn't say how long they'd been hiking when he stopped for a water break, but it was long since dark. She had no idea if they were on public or private land—one could get them shot. Of course, his friend would provide a location that wasn't easy to get to. If it wouldn't have been too noisy, she would have asked for a chopper ride.

As it was, her legs burned. The workout from earlier in the day might not have been the best idea considering she'd pushed herself. Then again, she'd been under the impression they were going to stay locked inside a cushy private home until it was time for the trial. Or driving to their next stop.

Lesson learned.

She should have known something like this would end up happening. At least it was cold enough to keep the mosquitoes away. Making this trek during the spring or summer months would have gotten her eaten alive.

Brewer leaned toward her, whispered, "Listen carefully to anything that sounds out of the ordinary. We're close."

"Okay." She could see his face clearly now that her eyes had adjusted to the darkness.

He turned and moved, slowly, methodically, deeper into the trees.

Crystal did her best not to make unnecessary noise. She'd turned down the lighting on her screen and put her phone on silent not long after they started the trek.

Brewer froze. He knelt down, indicating she should do the same without taking his eyes off whatever he'd seen up ahead. Did they find it? Was Trent here?

Crystal followed suit, reaching for and then palming her backup weapon. The SIG Sauer fit in her hand easily and provided a decently accurate shot. All bullets killed the same when they struck in the right place. In this case, size made no difference.

Brewer held a hand behind him, indicating she should stay put. So, she did as he disappeared into the thicket to their left. No doubt he would circle the perimeter. Minutes later, there was no sign of Brewer. No sound either.

For a split second, she feared this was it. This was the time he would ditch her in the woods and leave her to her own devices in the name of keeping her safe. The man could circle back to the vehicle and disappear for all she knew. Could he hot-wire a car? She had no idea but didn't doubt his skills for one minute. Doubting a man like Brewer would be a mistake. Underestimating the soldier in him wouldn't be smart.

And then she heard voices. Not much more than a whisper at first.

The sounds of movement alerted her to the fact Brewer at the very least was heading her way. Should she hide? What if it wasn't Brewer? What if he'd been stabbed and this was Trent? What if Trent was in league with other men and they accounted for the voices, not Brewer?

Crystal ran through all the possibilities, decided for better or worse she needed to move. She could gauge the reaction of whoever was coming once they arrived. So, she climbed the tree before they could get too close. From her vantage point, she would be able to get a visual on who was with Brewer before they knew where she was.

The thought that he could be in trouble, walking toward her with a gun to his back, struck. She dismissed the notion. Brewer wouldn't lead someone directly to her. He would lead the person the other way and then strike the second he believed he had an advantage. Brewer had the kind of patience that won wars. If he was walking her way with someone, he'd deemed the encounter to be safe.

Still, she would wait to see with her own eyes before making a decision to reveal herself.

The scent of pine tickled her nostrils. It dawned on her that she was allergic and it was only a matter of time before she sneezed. She'd been fine on the ground since it was cold outside. Grandma Lacy had moved to fake trees after Crystal's allergies had gotten so bad she couldn't be in the same room with the Christmas tree. To this day, Crystal lit a pine-scented candle to make it feel like Christmas in the small apartment where she resided.

This seemed an odd time for her to realize she hadn't felt the Christmas spirit in years. She lit the candle and put a wreath on her door, but that was the extent of her decorations. Growing up at the paint-horse ranch, the holidays had been magical.

More of that regret for abandoning her grandparents these last few years strangled her, causing her throat to close up.

Or maybe it was the smell of pine doing the trick. Either

way, the jig was about to be up. Crystal took in a long, slow breath and then held it, praying she wouldn't sneeze. Would it give her enough time to assess the threat?

Chapter Twenty-Two

A sudden sneeze drew Brewer's attention to the trees. He clamped his mouth shut and put a hand on Trent's chest to stop his friend from overreacting.

"Crystal?" he whispered as fear gripped him. He's been certain that she would still be in this spot.

"Here," came the familiar voice—a voice that dropped his pulse back to near-normal levels. She must have panicked when he hadn't immediately returned.

She climbed down and then sneezed again.

"This is Trent," he said once she'd settled down.

"I'm Marshal Remington," she said, taking the hand being offered.

"It's good to meet you," Trent said. "Looks like the cavalry has finally arrived."

"Where's your family?" Brewer asked.

"Safe," he responded. "For now."

Those were two words no person wanted in the same sentence when it came to protecting their family members.

"Your aunt must be—"

"Somewhere she won't easily be found," Brewer said, cutting Trent off. "Shall we head back to the car?"

"Sure," Crystal said. "What's the plan now?"

"Once we get back into cell range, I was thinking your superior could provide a safe house out here," Brewer said.

"How about we find a fishing cabin to spend the night in?" Crystal said. "According to the map, there are several lakes around."

Trent was shaking his head. "Bad idea. We should definitely get back to civilization."

"Why is that?" she asked.

"We can't stay in one place for too long," Trent quickly said. A little too quickly?

"Maybe we can join your family," Brewer stated. It was probably all the talk from Crystal about not knowing whether or not they could trust Trent that had Brewer questioning his friend's motives. His buddy hadn't done anything so far to cause alarm. Brewer would keep an eye on the situation, though. If Trent made a wrong move, they would leave him on the side of the road to fend for himself.

"Another bad idea," Trent said.

"I need your phone," Crystal said to him.

"My what?"

"You heard me," she said, calm as anyone pleased. "It's protocol. We can't risk anyone tracing us."

Trent's gaze bounced from Crystal to Brewer. Was he looking for some kind of intervention on Brewer's part? Because after what had happened, Trent would be waiting a long time. "Is that really necessary?"

"After reaching out to you with a new cell, our location was compromised," Crystal said matter-of-factly. "Now that might have been a coincidence, and for your sake, I'm hoping it was. But I'm not taking another chance like that."

If Trent's phone had been compromised, Crane's people should have been able to find them all this time.

"Okay, okay," Trent said a little more defensively than Brewer would have liked.

"What's the big deal?" he asked. "Hand over the phone."

"When will I get it back?" Trent asked. "I have a family to think about. If my wife can't get a hold of me, she'll panic."

His reasoning was solid. Keeping in touch with his family would explain why Trent hesitated to give his phone over. A twinge of guilt stabbed Brewer for not trusting his buddy's intentions. Trent stood to lose people close to him too.

"Once this is all over, you'll be welcome to retrieve it from the gas station bathroom where I intend to hide it," Crystal said.

Brewer leaned in so only she could hear. "Is that necessary? The man has a family to consider."

Crystal took a step back and caught his gaze. "Then let's do everything in our power to get him home safely so he can be reunited with his loved ones."

He couldn't argue her point, so he turned to his friend. "This is the best way for now."

Trent studied Brewer. His face morphed. "I shouldn't complain, man. I know. I still can't believe I got you into this mess in the first place. I guess my family will be safer if they can't get a hold of me until this is all behind us."

"That's the right attitude," Brewer said. "We'll get through this together. In the meantime, Crys... Marshal Remington has done a damn fine job keeping me alive." He put a hand out like he was presenting himself to the world. "I'm still here despite a few close calls and against the odds."

"Teamwork, Mr. Brewer," Crystal said, switching back to being formal.

Brewer's chest deflated a little even though he understood the need for them both to be as professional as possible now that Trent was in the picture.

Trent handed over his cell so the three of them could get on the move. Crystal tucked it inside her left pocket after turning the power off. Brewer doubted that would help in terms of security, but it might keep Trent from panicking if a call came through once they hit a patch with service.

"That's not all, sir." Crystal shot a look of apology to Brewer before shifting her gaze back to Trent. "I'm going to need to pat you down."

"You better believe I'm carrying," Trent stated, lifting his hands in the air. "And we're on the same team here."

"Even so, sir. It's protocol," she informed, her voice steady, even, and authoritative. "Nothing personal."

Trent shot a look at Crystal that could freeze water in hell before slowly turning his back, spreading his legs, and anchoring his hands against the nearby tree trunk. "You'll find a Glock tucked into a holster in the waistline of my jeans. That's all I have on me."

Brewer noted how formal Crystal was with Trent as she patted him down. Her guard was way up when it came to his military buddy. Did she have good reason?

Deciding an extra layer of precaution never hurt, Brewer filed the information under the *interesting* category and moved on. He would keep an eye on Trent too. The man was a bundle of jitters and nerves. Under the circumstances, it was understandable. Crystal might've been making a mountain out of a molehill. Either way, they were covered.

Crystal thanked Trent. "Do you need to pack up any supplies at your campsite before we head back to my vehicle?"

"Nah," he said. "I'll just leave everything here. No reason to waste time, and there's nothing that can't be replaced or retrieved at a later time."

"All right, then," she said, nodding to Brewer before turning the direction they'd come and hoofing it back.

It was past midnight by the time they located the car.

"Think we should grab a few hours of sleep before heading out?" Brewer asked, thinking of Crystal. They'd slept last night. In fact, he tried to forget just how right she'd felt in his arms and how fast and hard he'd fallen asleep. He couldn't remember the last time he'd slept so well.

"I'm good," Crystal said quickly. "I'll drive. You can do whatever you want in the back seat."

"I'm riding shotgun," Brewer argued.

"Not this time, champ," she said. Was it easier for her to keep an eye on Trent in front?

Crystal's moves were always tactical, so he didn't put up an argument. It would be easier for him to subdue Trent from the back seat, though.

"We'll both ride in back," he said, making a production out of opening the door for his friend.

Trent nodded, did as told. There was no humor in his eyes. Was he concerned about what would happen to his family if they were found?

Crystal claimed the driver's seat, then placed Trent's cell inside the console.

"Man, I'm just so glad you found me," Trent said to Brewer.

"How long were you waiting?" Brewer asked.

"Not long," he supplied. "Since last night after I stashed my family away. What about your aunt?"

"Same."

"She's good, though?" Trent continued.

"In good hands," Brewer stated.

"I sent someone to check on her, and they reported back that she wasn't home," Trent stated. He leaned back in the seat and swiped a hand over his face. "I've been worried sick ever since I tried to call you back and got nothing." He motioned toward Crystal and lowered his voice. "I'm guessing she's to blame for your phone going missing."

Brewer wasn't sure how he wanted to play this. On the one hand, he could pretend to be the victim here in a *good cop, bad cop* way. Trent already didn't like Crystal. It was obvious from his expression every time he looked at her and his reaction to her demand to turn over his cell.

But did they have more to worry about than Trent not being able to get in touch with his family? Or was there someone else waiting on a call?

THE PIT STOP at the gas station hadn't taken long. Crystal had hidden Trent's phone and was now the only person who knew the exact location of the cell. It was neater that way, especially when it came time to retrieve the piece of tech.

At this point, she was the only one with a cell. Hers had bars again, so she was finally in range for service. She had several texts from family members that she'd scrolled through while Brewer filled the gas tank. No news wasn't exactly good news when it came to a loved one being in a coma for an extended period of time.

The text exchange had been her siblings and cousins checking in. Since all six worked in different districts for the US Marshals Service, their jobs weren't nine-to-fives. They had to be ready to travel at a moment's notice when a felon was located or believed to be located because you never really knew until you arrived on scene.

One look at Brewer said he was relieved they'd found Trent. She didn't have history with the man, so there was no attachment for her, making it easier to be objective. Brewer was intelligent. He had street smarts. Under normal circumstances, she would trust his judgment on a person. He seemed to have the ability to read others well. Bias might get in the way, though.

Back on the road, she wondered if they could make a detour through Mesa Point on their way to the next safe house. Being a caring granddaughter was beginning to win over following exact protocol despite her need for perfectionism in her work. Crystal's SO needed time to find a good location. Elise wanted them closer to Austin, so she'd thrown out Round Rock as a possibility. The sprawling suburb north of Austin could be a good place to blend in.

Another front entry garage–type house would work until Elise figured out what she wanted to do with Trent, now that she was aware he was along for the ride. The best news so far was that Aunt Rosemary was in an upscale nursing home having the time of her life. Not even the promise of hot firemen would be able to pry her out, according to sources. It was a good place to tuck her away until this whole ordeal was over.

Then what?

Crystal hadn't given Brewer the sales pitch for WITSEC just yet. The subject had been brought up. The thought of Brewer disappearing, gaining a new identity and new life, sat hard on her chest.

The other message she hadn't seen fit to return was from Mahone.

I miss us.

Those three words twisted up her insides. She'd been clear. He wasn't *the one*. He needed to move on for his own sake. He deserved to find someone who could love him back. During their relationship, Crystal had believed she was broken somehow, that she was incapable of loving anyone. Was it the curse of her father's DNA? How much could he have loved her mother if the man couldn't stick around to bring up their children after she'd died giving birth?

Until meeting Brewer—and it was ridiculous when she really thought about it because the kiss had been so short—she'd thought what she'd had with Mahone was as far as she could go.

Her ex deserved better than mediocre feelings toward him. Crystal cared about him, but that wasn't the same thing as being the cliché head-over-heels in love with someone. The kind of love that made her stomach free-fall when he was near. The kind of love that made her so in tune with his presence, she knew the second he walked into a room. The kind of love that caused an electrical storm in the space between them and fire to burn low in her belly and warm the insides of her thighs.

Now that she'd experienced those things, there was no going back. Which was also ironic because there was no going forward with the only man who'd ever made her feel that way either.

"I might as well grab some sleep while I'm in good company," Trent said, shifting down in his seat farther, reminding her of a sullen teen. He tucked his chin to his chest and folded his arms across his chest.

"Go ahead, man," Brewer stated. "We'll keep watch for anything out of the ordinary."

Trent's phone was back at the gas station, so he couldn't

be trying to make a secret call for help or to give away their location by slinking down in his seat. She'd patted him down but hadn't found a wire either.

Then again, devices could be small enough to miss. Could they trust Trent?

Chapter Twenty-Three

A text came through on Crystal's phone from her boss.
Brewer read it out loud.

New plan. Go to Waco.

"That's it? That's all she says?" Crystal asked.

"Hold on," he said as three dots appeared on the screen.
Then, a link to an address. "She sent a link to a hotel."

He tapped on the link and rattled off directions.

"Guess my SO wants us to go antique shopping," she
quipped before glancing at Trent through the rearview and
buttoning up the look on her face. He must have shot a
look of confusion because she added, "Magnolia Market."
She studied him for a couple of seconds in the rearview.
"C'mon. Don't tell me you haven't heard of Chip and Jo-
anna Gaines."

He shrugged.

"Seriously?" she asked. Then came, "Oh, right. You've
been out of the country and then probably not in the mood
to care about a home-renovation show even if it swept the
country for a while."

"Can't say that I have," he admitted. "Or that I care."

She feigned disgust, and it made him chuckle. Brewer

missed the easy way they had with each other, but he needed to ensure Trent's safety. Until when? Would Damon punish Trent for being with Brewer? Hurt the man's family to prove a point?

Damon might get backlash from others for going that deep. Trent might've been fair game because he'd been the one who recommended Brewer to the job. Not on Brewer's watch. He would ensure his friend was safe. Maybe even cut a deal with Crystal to be one hundred percent certain of the fact.

From Palestine, the drive was a little less than two hours long. By the time they reached Waco, the sun was coming up. Brewer was wide awake. Trent, on the other hand, was snoring.

Crystal pulled behind a newer-looking hotel. She parked next to the service entrance. After sending a text, she cut off the car engine. As if on cue, a worker opened the back door and then waved them in. "Do you want to wake Sleeping Beauty over there?"

Brewer stifled a laugh. "On it."

He shook Trent, who immediately made a move to wrestle him. In a heartbeat, Crystal had her weapon drawn and pointed at the center of Trent's chest.

"Calm down, Trent. It's me. Brewer."

Trent mumbled a curse as his eyes blinked opened and he seemed to realize where he was. The look he shot Crystal for having a gun pointed at him would have scared most. She didn't budge.

"Everything okay back there?" she asked.

"Yeah, fine," he mumbled. "Now get the barrel away from me."

"As long as we're all good, I don't have a problem with

that." She eased the weapon down before holstering it. "Ready?"

"Where are we?" Trent asked through a yawn, looking disoriented.

"I'll tell you all about it inside," Brewer said, wishing he could check on his aunt. He'd feel a whole lot better if he could hear her voice, know that she was doing well.

The trio exited the vehicle and headed upstairs. They were led through the employee hallways to a room near the exit. No doubt this had all been planned out by Crystal's superior. The fact calmed Brewer's nerves slightly.

"I'll bring breakfast," the employee said. He didn't introduce himself, but he seemed to know Crystal when he touched her arm and asked to speak to her privately.

Brewer didn't like it.

"PLEASE TELL ME you didn't volunteer for this assignment," Crystal said to Mahone.

"Is it wrong that I want to know you're safe?" he asked.

"No," she answered. "But interfering with my case crosses a line."

"We're not together anymore," he countered. "Unless…"

"Same answer as before." Crystal needed to shut this down before Mahone got any more ideas. Letting him go down that path, giving him hope, would only hurt him more in the long run. Besides, she needed all her focus to make it through until Monday morning. "The last thing I want to do is hurt you. Believe me when I say I'd only hurt you more if we tried to keep this thing alive. I can't do that to you and understand if you don't want to be friends."

Mahone's face was turning redder by the second. Crystal hated being the one to do this to him.

"I need to get back into the room," she said. "Tomorrow's the big day, and neither one of us slept last night. I have to stay sharp."

"Fine," he said, but his attitude said he was angry.

She'd been honest. She hadn't led him on once she'd realized the relationship meant more to him than it did to her. She'd let him down as easily as humanly possible. Beyond that, there wasn't much else she could do.

"But this is not over," he mumbled as he turned to walk away.

Crystal exhaled a long, slow breath before heading back to the room. A distraction right now was the last thing she needed. She glanced at the time, performed a quick calculation in her head. Twenty-five hours and ten minutes to go.

The blackout curtain was pulled closed, the coffee machine percolating and brewing. The TV was on.

Shoes on, Trent took up the bed closest to the door. Should Crystal see it as an omen? His legs were crossed as he flipped through channels.

Brewer stood, leaning against the wall next to the coffee maker. "The first cup is ready." He motioned toward a full cup sitting next to the machine. "It's yours if you want it."

There was so much she wanted to say but couldn't. Hell, she didn't even know if it would be welcomed by Brewer. She would start with the fact she hadn't asked for Mahone to be assigned to this case. Nor did she want him here. Being defensive in front of Trent was a bad call. She took the coffee and settled on "Thanks."

Then there was the issue of Trent. She didn't trust the man. Nothing personal. She was doing her job—a job that had trained her to be suspicious of people first and trust them later. The trust part was a work in progress.

"Do you want to grab a few hours of sleep after breakfast arrives?" she asked Brewer.

"Not hungry," he supplied. "I had a power bar while you were in the hallway. It'll get me through until we can order a pizza or figure something out."

"Room service is going to provide meals," she said. "We're less than two hours from Austin, though traffic is unpredictable, so…" She glanced at the clock and performed another mental calculation. "We'll be safe if we leave by five o'clock in the morning."

"That leaves us a lot of time to play with," Brewer said.

"Maybe we should go over how this is going to go down." Plans had a way of changing in the heat of the moment, but it was good to have one at least.

She heard the toilet running in the next room, figured Trent—who looked a little too comfortable on the bed— had taken care of business while Brewer had made coffee.

"Go ahead." Brewer's voice was as stiff as his body language. Once this was over and he'd safely been delivered to court, could she talk to him about the possibility of seeing each other again off the job?

Or had she been reading too much into their bond? At least the bond she'd picked up on before meeting up with Trent. Now Brewer was cold as ice.

A knock at the door startled them. She immediately reached for her weapon, as did Brewer. Reflex?

It was most likely Mahone at the door with food.

"I've got this," she said, moving to the door before checking the peephole. Sure enough, he stood behind a room service cart on the other side.

Crystal opened the door. "I can bring this inside on my own."

Mahone nodded. "I'll be around in case you need me."

Having backup was probably a good idea. She would rest easier tonight. Rest? Crystal rolled her eyes. The final hours were the hardest in tough cases. Time seemed to slow to a drip. And she couldn't sleep until she'd delivered her package safely.

After thanking Mahone and requesting their next meals arrive around one o'clock, she took the cart and brought it inside. Everything smelled amazing, but she picked at her plate. Her stomach was queasy, but that didn't stop her from finishing her coffee. Without it, she highly doubted she would survive.

Trent passed out again. The man was awfully comfortable. But then, he trusted Brewer. The feeling was mutual despite evidence.

They watched back-to-back movies and one of those comedy specials on pay-per-view. Neither did much laughing, but the comedian's voice was better than silence. It was a decent enough distraction.

Brewer had been sitting there, quietly stewing. His mind was somewhere else altogether. And then he sat up ramrod straight. "Something has been bothering me, but I couldn't figure out what it was."

"Go on," she urged. She'd been having a similar feeling, but that wasn't uncommon in a case like this one.

"It just dawned on me what the problem is," he said, glancing over at a still-sleeping Trent. "He wasn't worried about calling his family on his cell."

The pieces all fit together for her now. The fact that Brewer had been found after making a call to Trent meant the man's line had been traced. "He should be very worried about Damon finding his family. But he was downright angry that I took his cell."

Brewer raked a finger through his hair.

"What did you do when I was out in the hallway with my coworker?" She lowered her voice on the last part and caught Brewer's gaze.

"Made coffee," he said. His pupils dilated as it dawned on him that Mahone was a marshal.

"Anything else?" she asked.

His eyes lit up. "Used the restroom."

"Leaving Trent alone with a landline," she supplied. "We have to get out of here."

"What about him?"

Trent sat up. "What about me?"

A knock at the door caused them both to jump. It occurred to Crystal that Trent was the only one who wasn't startled by the sudden noises. She drew her weapon and headed to the door with Brewer behind her for reinforcement.

Checking the peephole, she saw Mahone with more food. Crystal checked the time. It was close to one o'clock.

"Right. Food," Brewer said.

She opened the door. A random foot wedged inside. In the next second, a man came into view. With one hand, he wrapped his fingers around Crystal's neck as cold metal pressed to her forehead.

"Don't shoot." Brewer raised his hands in the surrender position.

"Set your weapon down," Damon ordered.

Crystal glanced over at Mahone, who shot a look of apology. Trent, the bastard, walked up behind Brewer and took his weapon.

"Sorry, man," Trent said. "It was you or me, and I have a family to think about."

"You're a sonofabitch," Brewer ground out. "I trusted you because of the bond I shared with the others in my unit. You didn't deserve it. You don't deserve the loyalty I've given you. And you sure as hell don't deserve to be treated like one of us. You're a damn traitor to the promises we all made to each other overseas. I hope you rot in hell."

Crystal wanted to scream. She glanced over at Mahone, who gave a slight nod at the food-service table that he was still gripping with both hands. She instantly knew what he was going to do.

In the next second, he rammed it into the back of Damon before the man could take Crystal's weapon. Her Krav Maga training kicked in.

In one swift movement, she brought her hand up as the cart rammed into Damon. The move caught him off guard. She took advantage of the moment to snatch his weapon from his hand and turn it on him instead.

Brewer fired off a headbutt. The crack against Trent's forehead echoed. He groaned and then dropped to his knees as blood from his now-broken nose splattered everywhere. A second later, Brewer had already spun around and managed to get his weapon back.

He used the butt of the gun to deliver a knockout hit.

Trent fell to the floor and slumped on his side.

Mahone pinned Damon to the wall. "Get out of here. Now!"

"Will you be—"

"Okay?" he asked. "Damn right I will be. Now, go!"

Brewer had her bag and his rucksack, urging her into the hallway before she could argue.

"I owe you one," she said.

Mahone smiled before handcuffing Damon, finally getting the message they could only ever be coworkers and friends.

She and Brewer bolted down the stairs and out the employee entrance. She claimed the driver's seat as Brewer scrambled into the passenger side.

As he pulled his seat belt over his chest and then locked it into place, she pulled out of the parking lot and onto 35. "Get my SO on speaker. We have to get him some help."

The call was quick. Mahone already had hotel security by his side. More help was on the way. All was under control.

"The only thing left to do is get your witness to the courtroom on time," Elise informed.

"Yes, ma'am," Crystal promised. "I'm headed there now to be close to the courthouse. Any chance we can have early access to the building?"

"I'll see what I can do," Elise promised.

Waco to Austin was a three-hour drive with late afternoon traffic despite the distance on maps. Crystal found paid parking on the street three blocks from the courthouse.

They stayed there until half an hour before time to report when the text came from her SO indicating they would have assistance. Four squad cars encased them as they made the short drive to the courthouse.

"So this is what it feels like to be president," Brewer stated, smiling for the first time in what felt like days. "I think I'll pass."

They pulled up to the front of the courthouse, where they were met with a squad of officers.

"This is where we part ways," she said to him. "Go in there and put the bastard away with your testimony. Okay?"

"I'll do my best," he said before reaching over and running his finger along the back of her hand. It shouldn't have been as sexy as it was. "Will you be out here when I'm done?"

"Maybe," she said. "I have something to take care of."

Brewer nodded, saluted, and then disappeared into the small army of officers escorting him inside.

Epilogue

Two days later

"Do I have your word?" Crystal had no plans to hang up this call without confirmation. There was too much at risk.

"You do."

"Thank you," she said into the receiver. "I only wish I could have been the one to set it up. Hear the words, the commitment with my own ears."

"You know you can trust me. Right?"

"Of course," Crystal stated. "With my life."

"Good. Do me a favor."

"Anything," she promised.

"Go see your family and forget about this place for a while."

"That's a deal," Crystal said before adding, "What happened to the bounty hunters?"

"Larson Figgs is going down for attempted murder," Elise informed. "The woman is known as The Widow for her proclivity to wear all black, and was last seen heading over the border to Mexico. I imagine she'll stay there until the situation cools off. We'll catch her when she attempts to cross over again."

"Good," Crystal said. "Both need to be locked up."

"Agreed," Elise said. "I had Mahone pick up Trent's cell from the gas station and admit it into evidence. There's nothing left for you to do except go take that time off."

"Will do," Crystal said. "I'll take care of informing Wade Brewer of the update."

She ended the call with her SO after perfunctory good-byes and then walked into the private room in the court-house where she knew Wade would be. "It's over," she said to him. "Really over. You did your part, and the jury will send this bastard away for a very long time."

He sighed relief as he studied her. Then came, "They'll come for me when I'm not looking. I'll never be safe as long as I'm on the grid. And since I can't leave Aunt Rosemary alone, I'm a dead man walking." He shrugged, looked re-signed.

"There's another solution," Crystal said. "But before I tell you, I'd like to inform you that you're no longer my witness. You can walk out that door anytime."

Wade crossed the room. She took a step back and an-chored herself against the wall. And then she grabbed a fistful of his shirt and tugged him toward her until their lips were barely an inch apart. "Does that mean what I think it does?"

"I hope so," she said, smiling. "You did it, Wade. You testified. From what I hear Crane is going to be locked up for a very long time. Damon will be sent to a different prison, as will Trent."

Wade's gaze locked onto hers, causing a literal fire-works show to explode inside her chest. "I wasn't sure I'd ever see you again."

She swallowed to ease some of the sudden dryness in her throat to no avail.

"You have quite the effect on me, Wade," she said, staring into eyes filled with the same ache she felt.

"You called me Wade," he pointed out, surprised.

"I guess I did," she admitted.

"That's a big deal for you," he said.

She smiled and said, "Yes, it is."

"I'd like permission to kiss you," he said.

"Granted," was all she said before his lips came crashing down on hers. He kissed her with the kind of intensity that lit a wildfire inside her. She parted her lips for him after his tongue tested the barrier.

He tasted like a mix of dark-roast coffee and peppermint toothpaste...better than Christmas morning.

Wade closed the gap between them, his body flush with hers, her back against the wall. She brought her hands up to his shoulders to anchor herself as she got lost in the kiss.

She dropped her hand to the center of his chest and could feel his rapid heartbeat against her palm.

A noise in the hallway brought them back to reality too fast.

Wade pressed his palm against the wall as he rested his forehead against hers. They both tried to calm their rapid breathing. "I have to go soon."

"You don't," Crystal said. "Not if you don't want to."

He drew his head back and caught her gaze. "I think we both know the hand I've been dealt."

"Yes," she began, "but what if I was able to reshuffle the deck?"

"I'd have to hear you out, wouldn't I?"

"I already mentioned that Michael Mylett's son was arrested for aggravated assault," she stated.

"Ri-i-i-ght."

"My SO was able to negotiate on your behalf," Crystal

continued, unfazed. She could scarcely wait to tell him the news. "In exchange for lessening the charges against his son to essentially a slap on the wrist, we were able to get a commitment from Mylett that no one would harm you or your aunt. You'll be under his protection for life."

Wade stood there for a long moment, his expression unreadable stone.

"I thought you'd be happy," Crystal said, confused by his reaction.

"What if I don't want to be under his protection?" he asked.

Crystal wasn't sure what about the arrangement didn't make sense to him. "No, this is a good thing. Mylett is the top dog now that Crane's been arrested. No one will go against him. You'll be safe to walk down the street and do as you please."

Wade's lips compressed. Was he frowning?

She brought her hands up to cup his face, deciding to put her heart on the line. "We could see each other, if you'd like."

Wade shook his head. Her heart fell, landing with a *thud*. "I thought you—"

He shushed her by covering her mouth with his and kissing her so thoroughly that she almost forgot where she was.

Was it a kiss goodbye?

"The reason I'm not okay with the arrangement is because if I'm under anyone's protection, I want it to be yours." Wade broke into a wide smile. "I've spent a long time on this earth without even realizing someone like you existed. I never believed in love at first sight until I met you. Because you proved to me that I can trust my eyes. I may not be able to hear out of both ears, and I don't have..." He motioned toward his prosthetic leg. "All of me. But what's left belongs to you. Heart and soul. I mean it, Crystal. I've dated enough people to know when I've found the real deal. It's you. I fell in love with you. And there's no one else I'd rather be with than you. For life."

"You might not see yourself as a whole person anymore, Wade. But I do," Crystal said, tears gathering in her eyes. "Because what really makes a person whole is their heart. Their brains. Their mind. The mold was broken when you were made. But you weren't broken when the mold was damaged." Crystal stared up into the eyes of the man she loved. "We're all damaged in some way or another, Wade. I'm not perfect. You'll figure that out soon enough. What counts, what makes a whole person is what's in here." She placed the flat of her palm against his heart. "You're whole. You're perfect. I'm madly in love with you. Only you. It's only ever been you."

Wade picked her up off her feet and kissed her.

"Promise me one thing," she said when they broke apart.

"Anything," he said. "Name it."

"You'll give me your heart forever," she said.

"It's yours," he said. "Before we even met, my heart belonged to you. I just didn't know it until I met you."

"Good." She beamed. "Because I'm asking for forever."

"On one condition," he countered.

"Okay," she said.

"Forever starts today."

A rogue tear streaked down her cheek. Wade dipped his head and kissed it. He feathered kisses on her eyelids, the tip of her nose, her chin, until finding her lips.

Wade pulled back first. "Should we head to Mesa Point after picking up Aunt Rosemary?"

Crystal laughed. She felt lighter than she could remember. It would change when she got to Mesa Point. She realized the heaviness in her chest would return. And that was okay. Finding happy moments was even more important to her as she realized how truly fragile life could be. But that wasn't why she'd laughed. "I got an update on your aunt."

"Oh?"

"Turns out she started a wet T-shirt contest for the male orderlies," she said, covering her laugh with her hand.

Wade's laugh was a low rumble in his chest. Sexy as hell. And now hers.

"Sounds about right," he finally said. "Guess we should give her another night or two in paradise."

"I think she'd appreciate that," Crystal said as she reached for his hand. He was reaching for hers at the same time. Their fingers met in the middle.

It was time to go. To get out of the courthouse. To start living.

And it was time to go home to Mesa Point, where the rest of her heart resided. With Wade by her side, she could weather any storm. This man was her lifeline, and she couldn't wait to spend the rest of their lives together, side by side, as partners and equals.

"By the way, when you said you were playing for forever, I hope you meant it because I fully intend to ask you to marry me," Wade said, causing her heart to sing.

"I don't need a piece of paper to prove this is the kind of love that will last a lifetime," she said. "But a wedding is a good place to start."

* * * * *

Look for more books in
USA TODAY *bestselling author Barb Han's*
miniseries Marshals of Mesa Point
coming soon.

And if you missed the first title, you'll find
Ranch Ambush
wherever Harlequin Intrigue books are sold!